L L.

THE KNOCKER ON DEATH'S DOOR

The knocker hung on a very special door – oak, heavy, with a late-Gothic arch, and apparently a late-Gothic curse. Then the door was moved from an old house, once an abbey, to the village church. Legend held that sinners who seized the knocker had their hands burned by the cold iron. But Gerry Bracewell didn't die of burns, neither did a second victim. Had they knocked on death's door, or was a more down-to-earth killer at large?

Detective Chief Inspector George Felse, returning from a weekend in Wales, had passed through the village of Mottisham and watched the ceremony enacted to re-dedicate the door. Little did he know that soon he would be called back to investigate murder . . .

THE KNOCKER ON DEATH'S DOOR

Ellis Peters

Macdonald

A Macdonald Book

Copyright © Ellis Peters 1970

First published in Great Britain in 1970
by Macmillan and Co., Ltd., London

This edition published in 1989 by
Macdonald & Co (Publishers) Ltd
London & Sydney

British Library Cataloguing in Publication Data

Peters, Ellis, *1913*–
   The knocker on death's door.
   Rn: Edith Pargeter
   I. Title
   823'.912 [F]

   ISBN 0–356–17592–8

Printed in Great Britain by
Redwood Burn Limited, Trowbridge, Wiltshire
Bound at the Dorstel Press

Macdonald & Co (Publishers) Ltd
66–73 Shoe Lane
London EC4P 4AB

A member of Maxwell Pergamon Publishing Corporation plc

CHAPTER 1

THE DOOR was of oak, roughly five feet wide by more than seven feet high, with a top in the form of a flattened late-Gothic arch. The timbers from which it had been made, with loving care, some five hundred or more years ago, were nearly six inches thick, and carved on the outer side into crude vertical folds, and with the wear and tear of centuries, and the rigours of recent cleaning to remove the gloss of dirt from accumulated time and the touch of many hands, the colour of the wood had clarified into an exquisite matt brown fading away into pure grey, the colour of subdued light at the onset of evening after a clear day, and the grain to a veining of liquid silver, so that the carved folds were no longer related in any way to anything so solid as linen, but appeared rather as shot silk of a cobweb fineness. In certain lights the door seemed almost translucent, so that you might have tried to walk through it in the belief that it was mere mirage, and no more palpable than mist. Actually it weighed an inconscionable amount, and had elicited fervent curses from the modern workmen who had had the job of moving it. They were accustomed to the gim-crack soft-woods of today, and only one of them had so far forgotten himself as to stroke the silken meshes with a loving and wondering hand, and feel for a moment deprived and born out of time. He was an old man, of course, reared in the trade. The others thought it was simply a quarter of a ton of over-valued junk.

The crowning arch of the door had a carved border of leaves, undercut so deeply that they could almost have been plucked at will, though only by Titans. Beneath this canopy two elongated angels, hieratic and crude and modern now as Modigliani, though certainly years out of date when they were carved, spread large hands and rigid wings over the entering worshipper. Or, of course, butler, depending on the period in question, but reverence was always equally implied.

For the door had hung for centuries on the massive hinges of the wine-cellar in the house known as the Abbey, in the village of Mottisham, in West Midshire. It was now being restored to its ancient place (hypothetically, at least, for the actual evidence was slim and ambiguous) in the south porch of the church of Saint Eata in the above-named village. A very rare dedication indeed, and territorially limited, and if there was a person in the parish who had any very clear idea of who St. Eata was, it certainly was not the vicar, the Reverend Andrew Bright, who was thirty-one, and devoted to Rugby, God (or his extremely simple idea of God), rock-climbing, youth-clubs and his own advancement, in that order. He was himself, however, solid, worthy and real, and knew a real, solid, worthy work of art when he saw one. He had jumped at the offer of the door, and ruthlessly adapted the nineteenth-century south porch, the latest of many renovations to St. Eata's long-suffering fabric, to accommodate it. With the effect achieved he was more than content. It was a very beautiful, thought-provoking and virtually permanent door. That it had other and more disquieting properties was not yet apparent.

As for the knocker, it was of antique iron, rust-proof practically for ever, of a lovely, crude texture that gave acute tactile pleasure to anyone handling it.

The surface was not quite smooth, being very slightly pitted all over, so that it clung to the hand with a live, bracing contact. It was made in the form of a beast's head, wreathed in leaves that never grew on any tree, as the beast had never roamed in any jungle but that of Apocalypse; and in the wide, generous, patently amiable jaws was proffered, rather than gripped, a large, twisted ring of iron, thick enough to fill the palm.

Through this door the bishop emerged, radiant and serene, beautifully robed and crozier in hand, at the conclusion of the service, with the Reverend Andrew and the living representatives of the Macsen-Martel family at his heels, on his way to the vicarage for tea with muffins, scones and fruit cake, suitable to an English Sunday. Traffic on the B road through the village was halted to allow his procession to make its way across the green with becoming dignity and deliberation, which took some time. The village itself looked on from a discreet distance, tolerantly un-smiling and unfrowning, missing not a trick. Com-paratively few of the inhabitants had been among the congregation inside St. Eata's. Mottisham was a reassuringly normal English village.

Motorists, impatient but resigned, sat back and waited for the magnificently aesthetic old man, less ingenuous than he appeared, to withdraw his train inside the confines of the vicarage grounds, a manoeuvre over which he took his time. Who knows when the arrested mind will open and the light dawn?

Detective Chief Inspector George Felse and his wife Bunty were on their way back from a week-end by the Welsh coast; probably the last of the year, for it was mid-October and the best of the weather was already gone. They had left immediately after lunch, to avoid the normal concerted rush back to the Midlands, only to find that even more people than usual had been

visited by the same idea. The trouble with mid-
Wales is that the mountains render whole tracts of it
impossible for major, or indeed any, roads, and
confine the motorist to the few main arteries. The
inevitable boring, irritating, nose-to-tail procession
home was something George detested, but for many
miles could not escape. But towards the Midshire
border he swung thankfully off to the right, and took
the minor road that threaded the long cleft of
Middlehope, between the hills. It was longer, and
probably a few of the regular commuters to the Welsh
coast had discovered its advantages by now, but even
so it was a relief after the main road.

Through the few stark villages, with their half-
Welsh, half-English names, they made better time,
and had something better to look at than the butt-end
of the car in front. Road and river wound inextricably
along the valley, crossing and re-crossing in an
antique dance of their own. In some of those bridges
there was Roman masonry. There was even a short
stretch of Roman causeway still exposed at the
approach to one of them, perhaps twelve yards of
huge stones laid like crazy paving, none too smooth
even now, after centuries of weathering. Those who
knew the road slowed to a crawl and shambled over
them with respect; the unwary from the cities hit them
at speed, and banged their heads on their car roofs at
the first bound. Strangers, hearing they were Roman,
assumed they had been carefully preserved for
archeological purposes. The truth was that in
Middlehope things survived; no one preserved them.
They had always been there, and were still serviceable, why move them?

Outside the narrow ribbon of level fields that
fringed the road, this was sheep country, and the
pastures rose steeply into rough slopes of grass and
heather, broken at the crests by a few outcrops of

rock. Gradually the red and white brick chapels of Wales gave place to the small, squat-towered stone churches of England. The bracken along the hills was already russet, the heather a brownish purple so dark as to match the occasional patch of bare, peaty soil. Sheep minced along the contours with slow, delicate movements, heads down, as deliberately as though they possessed the whole of time, the elders still showing the shapeliness of their summer clipping, the yearlings fat rolls of wool. Life did not change much in Middlehope. Why should it? The basic way of living here, in a hard but beautiful solitude, had been evolved long ago, and only minor adaptations had been made to them since.

Until they drew near to the village of Mottisham, that is. Along with several other similarly attractive places scattered round the rim of a ten-mile circle surrounding the county town of Comerbourne, Mottisham was just beginning to feel the effect of the progressive withdrawal of the wealthier townspeople from their town. The latest ripple of the expanding ring had only just reached them; but there in the opening bowl were the first two new estates, one of council houses but the other, more significantly, of that curious modern phenomenon, the "executive-type" dwelling. A few of the older houses at the edge of the village had also been taken over and done up by new and obviously well-to-do owners. And in the thin copse behind the churchyard half a dozen artfully deployed "desirable residences"—one step higher up the social scale—were just being built, so carefully arranged that no one should look into anyone else's windows, or, indeed, see anyone else's roof, and most of the trees should be retained in what would certainly be advertised as "picturesque wooded grounds".

The road made a great loop all round the church-yard, shrinking between old buildings; and there, stationed at the curve by "The Sitting Duck", was a white-gloved police sergeant, waving all traffic to a standstill with a palm the size of a spade. George pulled in obediently to the side and stopped. Within seconds there were three more cars drawn up behind him.

"Now what's going on?" he wondered aloud, and wound down the window to peer ahead. The sergeant, having secured the desired effect, rolled ponderously alongside and stooped to the obvious inquiry. The car was new, along with George's recent promotion, and country members of the constabulary had as yet no reason to associate a pale grey VW 1500 with the deputy head of the County C.I.D.

"Shan't be keeping you more than a few minutes, sir . . . " He did a double take with admirable equanimity, and continued in the same tone and the same tempo: "Well, well, I see I caught a big one. How are you, George? And Mrs. Felse, ma'am . . . we haven't seen you up this way for quite some time. How's the boy?" Sergeant Moon was a very old acquaintance, and but for the remoteness of his chosen solitude, now apparently becoming rapidly less remote, he would have ranked as a close friend.

"Fine, thanks, Jack!" Dominic was away in France with his fiancée, as it happened, recovering, he said, from post-examination exhaustion and pre-life cold feet, and considering for the first time entirely seriously and for the first time with trepidation, what he was to do with himself and his career. "How about your own family? Well, I hope?"

Sergeant Moon acknowledged the inquiry gravely; his wife and daughter were well. "You don't find us much to do up here. or you'd see more of us," George said. At the time this was a strictly truthful statement, but somebody somewhere was certainly listening, and took malicious note.

"Ah, that's right," acknowledged Sergeant Moon, leaning a sharp blue elbow on the VW's roof. "Crime, by and large, we don't go in for. A bit of riotous behaviour now and again, that's about it. Sin, now, sin's more in our line." The distinction was clear, thoughtful and comforting. The sins of Middlehope were time-honoured, the contrivances of an enclosed community still governed by pre-feudal sanctions, and generally speaking the sinners were disciplined by their own society and did not totally shirk responsibility for their acts. The sergeant knew where the law ought to restrain its hand and leave older laws to function, with profounder humanity and sounder common sense. "Today," he said, "we should be whiter than snow. We've got company."

"So I see," said George. "What exactly is going on?"

"You haven't been reading the ecclesiastical news and notes, have you? We've got the bishop, no less. Look out, here he comes!"

And here he came. The church, a square-towered conglomeration of seventeenth- and nineteenth-century renovations on the poor remnants of a very ancient foundation, lay on the left of the road, half-screened by old trees and ringed by its crowded graves. To the right, on the other side of the road, was the nineteenth-century vicarage, three-coloured brick with dozens of gables and mock-Gothic windows, a pretentious and unmanageable mess. It had, however, a generous and well-stocked garden with plenty of fruit trees. Towards this green shade the bishop took his unhurried way. He was undoubtedly impressive. All the women watching from windows, doorways and pavement touched their hair and smoothed their dresses at the sight of him. The word that entered George's head was "bridled". The word that entered Bunty's was "blossomed". Six feet tall and something over, fragile and ascetic as a primitive saint (and every bit as durable), with a fleshless face honed into an incredible refinement of benevolence and beauty, and longish silvery hair framing it, the bishop paced slowly along the flagged path, his frilled sleeves falling back from emaciated hands, posed exquisitely in the frame of the lych-gate for half a dozen photographers who materialised surprisingly out of nowhere in particular, and flowed majestically across the road towards his promised vicarage tea.

'If you're going to do a thing,' observed Sergeant Moon approvingly, ''I like to see it done well. These hearty modern clerics don't know they're born.''

''But what's he been up to?'' George wanted to know.

''Re-dedicating our south door. Hadn't you heard? It's been hung somewhere in the cellars of the Abbey ever since the dissolution of the monasteries, and now they've been clearing up the old place in the hope that the National Trust will take it over, they wanted to put back the things that were pinched, and get everything in order. Done a very nice restoration job on that door, so they tell me.''

The vicar, walking behind his bishop, was half a head shorter and about three times as wide, a burly young man with a round, ingenuous face and muscles befitting a wing three-quarter. A late shaft of sun bounced from his red hair like singed fingers recoiling from a burning bush.

''You've got the press on the run,'' said George. ''I never thought a door could bring in so many cameras!''

''It's said to be something special, all right. The experts got the word, apparently. The thing's never been on view before, you see. Nobody writes up the Abbey, not these days.''

"Nor the family?" said George curiously. "I take it that's the squire following on?"

"Don't mention that word here, George, we're allergic to it. Even if they used it at all, it would be about old Thwaites who bought up the Court fifty years ago—and if they used it about *him* it would have inverted commas round it, and nasty implications. We're tribal, not feudal. And even the old princes of Powis didn't venture to show their faces here unless they were invited."

"The lords of shop and bank are coming, by the look of your housing plans," said Bunty.

"Let 'em come, they'll learn. But, yes," he said, returning to the little procession which had just reached the vicarage gate, "that's Robert Macsen-Martel and his mother. Don't see her often these days. He works for Poole, Reed and Poole, in the estate office—talking of historical ironies, though I know we weren't. Sells expensive little gimcrack houses all round what's left of his own—and after all, they've been there best part of nine centuries. God knows how they stuck it out, they never were wealthy. Probably the best they ever did was out of that dissolution business, when the monks got kicked out. Count for nothing now. Never will again. Never *did*, for all that much."

It was an epitaph; and there was something about the two figures now vanishing into the vicarage garden that suggested that even the epitaph was an afterthought, long after the event of dissolution.

The old woman was exceedingly tall and ramrod erect, a residue of desiccated flesh shrunk tightly to attenuated bones, and draped with old-fashioned and shapeless tweeds of no particular colour. Under an ancient felt hat, worn dead straight on lank grey hair drawn into a bun on her neck, the long, narrow, aristocratic face looked out with chill disapproval at

the world, as though she had ceased to expect
anything good from present or future.

"She looks," said Bunty thoughtfully, "like that
bronze bishop at Augsburg—the one with the bad
smell under his nose."

"Bishop Wolfhart Roth," said Sergeant Moon
understandingly. "Now you come to mention it, so
she does." And it was entirely typical of him that he
should be able to haul out of his capacious memory
not only the face but even the name of a German
bishop some unknown artist had caricatured in
bronze in the fourteenth century.

Her son was like her, but not yet mummified. Tall,
thin, with long, narrow bones and a long, narrow
face, withdrawn, distrustful, austere. An uncomfort-
able family, Bunty thought, watching them disappear
under the vicar's trees, but too faded now to
discomfort the populace of Mottisham overmuch.

They were gone, it was over. The sergeant flapped
a huge white hand in a final salute, and withdrew to
his duty, waving the VW on towards home. Bunty
turned to stare into the porch as they passed by, and
try to catch a glimpse of the door that had brought
press photographers and scholars into the wild
territory of Middlehope. Old trees crowded close,
darkening the cavity of the porch. She caught a faint
flash of pale, pure colour, old wood restored to the
light from under the patina of centuries of dirt and
neglect; but that was all.

"Sorry!" said George. "Did you want to stop and
have a look at it? I couldn't hold up the procession,
but we can pull round into the pub yard if you like,
and walk back."

"No, never mind." Bunty settled back in her seat,
her thoughts returning pleasurably to the prospect of
getting home and getting the Aga lit and the house
warmed. "I don't suppose there's anything so re-

markable about it. Nothing to fetch us back for another look.''

Whatever minor fate had been jolted by George's assessment of the Middlehope crime potential, and Moon's acceptance of it, must also have recorded, and with the same malice, this complacent comment —probably under the category of famous last words!

There were still three reporters and one press photographer left over from the jamboree when Hugh Macsen-Martel and Dinah and Dave Cressett entered the public bar of ''The Sitting Duck'' that evening. Saul Trimble, trading on his antediluvian appearance as usual, had already lured two of the visitors into his corner, one on either side, and was furnishing them with a few impromptu fragments of folk-history in return for the pints with which, alternately, they furnished him. He had left out his false teeth for the occasion, which added twenty years to his appearance, and put on his old leather-elbowed jacket and a muffler instead of his usual smart Sunday rig. By good luck the bar itself still looked every inch the antiquated country pub for which it was cast, since Sam Crouch, who owned it, was too mean to spend money on modernising it, and had no need to worry about competition. There were two other pubs within reach, but both were tied, while ''The Sitting Duck'' was not merely a free house, but a home-brewed house into the bargain, one of only three left in the entire county. So the public bar was still all quarries and high-backed settles, furnished with bright red pew cushions, and every evening the place was full. This Sunday evening it was perhaps even a little fuller than usual. The newsmen, strangers from the town, were fair game, and there was the afternoon's show to talk about.

Saul was in full cry when Hugh's party entered. He

was using his folk-lore voice, half singing Welsh, half quavering, superstitious old age, and all the regulars were there to egg him on. William Swayne, alias Willie the Twig, the forestry officer from the plantations beyond the Hallowmount, had driven down in the Land-Rover, Eli Platt had closed his by-pass fruit and flower stands early, and come in from the market-garden on the fringe of Comerbourne, Joe Lyon, smelling warmly of his own sheep, steamed gently by the fire with a pint of home-brewed in one hand. It may even have been the beer, rather than the company, that had caused the strangers to prolong their visit into licensing hours.

"Normans?" Saul was saying with tremulous disdain. "Normans, is it? The Normans were mere incomers here, and never got a toehold, not in Middlehope, not for hundreds of years. The few that got in by marrying here, them we tolerated if they minded their step, the rest—out! Normans, indeed!"

"I was going by the name," said the oldest reporter reasonably.

"Martel? Oh, ah, that's Norman, that is. The Martel got in with one o' these marriages I was telling you about. In Henry One, that was, there was no sons to the family, and the heiress, she took up with this Martel, who was an earl's man from Comerbourne, but had fallen out with his master. Let him alone, they did, when he had the clans of Middlehope behind him, they wanted no extra trouble up on this border. Been Macsen-Martels ever since, they have, right enough, but they'd been here many a hundred years before that—ah, right back to King Arthur and the Romans afore him . . ."

"This," said Hugh in Dinah's ear, as he found her a chair in the bow window, "is going to be good." He caught Saul's impervious blue eye, bright beneath a deliberately ruffled eyebrow, and winked. Saul looked

through him stonily into the far distances of in-
spiration.

"I'll get them," volunteered Dave, and went off
through the crowd to the bar, where Ellie Crouch and
her nineteen-year-old daughter, christened Zenobia
but Nobbie to her friends, dispensed home-brewed
and presided over the scene like a couple of knowing
blonde cherubs, deceptively guileless of eye.

"If you'm going by names," pursued Saul,
warming almost into song, "it's the Macsen you want
to think about, my lads. You know who Macsen was?
He was the same person as Maximus, King of the
Britons, back in the fifth century. And if you don't
believe me, go and look for yourselves at the inscrip-
tion on the Pillar of Eliseg, up north there by Valle
Crucis, and there you'll see it in Latin . . ."

"Are you telling us you can read Latin?"
demanded the youngest reporter dubiously.

"Course I can't, nor never needed to, and if I
could, I couldn't make out the letters on that stone,
but there's those who have, and turned it into English
for you and me both. Look it up in the libraries!
'Maximus the King,' it says, 'who slew the King of
the Romans . . . ' Macsen Wledig, the Welsh called
him. And do you know who the King of the Romans
was, the one he slew? He was the Emperor Constans,
that's who, and uncle to King Arthur himself. And
ever since Macsen Wledig was Prince of Powis
there've been Macsens in Middlehope."

"How do you know?" objected the young reporter
boldly. "Are there still records of all this? After all
that length of time?"

"There's better than written records. There's the
records that have come down by word of mouth from
father to son and mother to daughter. Why, my old
granny could have recited you the pedigree of every
family in this village nearly back to Adam, just like in

the Bible. The women . . . the women were the keepers of the traditions ever since time started. Now that's all gone. Progress we've got, and it's cost us everything else we had, whether we wanted it or not . . . ''

"He's beginning to ramble," Dinah said softly. "Hadn't you better give him a shove back on to the rails?"

Someone else, however, did that in Hugh's place, and very effectively. The last of the photographers sat on a high stool at the end of the bar, a big, hearty man just running slightly to flesh, with a shock of untidy straw-coloured hair and inquisitive eyes. He hadn't been priming Saul, he hadn't been doing much talking, but it was plain that he had missed nothing.

"What about this door?" he said. "If it was originally one door of the church, how did it get into their house in the first place?"

Saul trimmed his sails nimbly, got half way through an unplanned sentence, decided to revise it, and created a mild diversion by peering meaningfully into his empty pint-pot. One of his two interlocutors took the hint and filled it again.

"It got there because they took it, along with a few other things, when the monastery here was closed down under Henry Eight, that's how. A very nice bit of carving it is, you can see that, and made locally, so the experts say, and there's bits inside the old part o' the church by the same hand. Closed down, the monastery was, and the brothers turned out on to the road. The abbey church was looted and abandoned for a while, and then it was took over for the parish church and repaired again. And the Macsen-Martels sided with the commission, they did, and they got the abbot's lodging to live in, and that's how the door came to be there."

"And what," the photographer wanted to know, "put it into their heads to give it back now? Nobody knew about it. Nobody was asking for it. Nobody was in any position to ask for it. Are you telling me they suddenly went to the trouble and expense of having the thing cleaned and restored, after all this time, just in a fit of belated honesty? It doesn't make sense.''

They all turned to look at him more carefully, for the tone of his questioning was curiously more purposeful than that of his colleagues. Dave came back with the drinks, and put Dinah's half-pint into her hand. Hugh levelled black eyes above the rim of his pint-pot. ''Who is he?'' he asked softly. ''Not a Comerbourne man, I know them all.''

''Brummagem, I think. Some freelance.'' Dave was uninterested; he didn't question other people's declared motives for what they did.

''Don't,'' warned Saul unexpectedly, his voice receding hollowly into a cavern of senile solemnity, ''don't ask me about that! There's reasons for wanting to have things—like a good cellar door when you're setting up house and there's one standing handy—and reasons for wanting not to have things any longer when they begin to turn malignant towards them that took them out of their right place. Don't forget 'tis a *church* door. Better for everybody, maybe, to put it back where it was afore, and have the bishop say the good words over it that it might be glad to hear. Mind, I'm not saying it *is* so, I've only said it *might* be so. I haven't even said it would be effective, have I? Just that there's no harm in trying.'' And he shook his grey head as though he foresaw the failure of this belated attempt at exorcism of something unnamed and undefined. ''Did you know what sort of monastery we had up here at the finish?'' he asked mildly. ''There were only four o' the brothers left to take to the roads, and a beggarly sort of place they kept here. Hospitality for the stranger, my eye! There were strangers slept here overnight that never got where they were going. It was a long way for any bishop to come, to see for himself what was going on. And then, bishops are as fond of sleeping safe as the next man. No, I wouldn't say Mottisham Abbey had a particularly holy reputation in its last days. Even the church, they say, saw some very odd goings-on before the finish.''

"Are you saying," demanded the photographer bluntly, "that there's something uncanny about that door?''

"I'm saying nothing, except that it's better to be safe than sorry," mumbled Saul darkly, "and back in the church is the best place for a door the like of that one. Don't you get too inquisitive, my lad, about things that's best let alone.''

"But *what* went on in the church?'' the youngest reporter pressed avidly. "Do you mean black masses, and things like that?''

"'Tisn't for me to say. There were tales . . . there were tales . . . '' The veiled eye and withdrawn manner implied that he had heard them all at first-hand, but didn't propose to share them.

"Oh, go on!" urged Willie the Twig, fixing Hugh across the smoky room with an innocent grey stare. "Tell 'em about the family curse. Tell 'em what happens in every third generation, ever since the Dissolution . . . ''

"Young man," said Saul weightily, playing for time while he readjusted to this uninvited assistance, "there's some things better not spoke of . . . ''

"Why?" asked Hugh with interest. "It won't just go away, whether you speak about it or not, every-body knows it happens.''

"Every third generation," prompted Willie the Twig gently.

"Ever since the last abbot was thrown out to beg,

and put a curse on the usurpers for all time . . . ''
confirmed Hugh. Dinah dug her elbow sharply into
his ribs, but he only smothered a small convulsion of
laughter in what was left of his beer, and looked
round to claim Dave's empty pint-pot. ''You, Dinah?
No? Here you are, Nobbie, love, same again!''

Saul's stony eye fixed him balefully. Hugh suppres-
sed his charming smile and gazed back in monumental and brazen innocence.

''But what *does* happen every third generation?''
the youngest reporter insisted.

''Every third generation,'' Saul said with vengeful
deliberation, and his voice sank into the cellar like the
demon king disappearing down a stage trap, ''the
second son is born a witless idiot.''

''Or a degenerate monster,'' Hugh added help-
fully.

''Go on, you're having us on!' Protested the
reporter.

''You think so? *You didn't see the second son at the
service this afternoon, did you?*'

'You *devil*!' whispered Dinah.

Hugh didn't even trouble to warn her to silence; he
knew she disapproved, or at the very best withheld
her approval, but he also knew she wouldn't do anything to spoil the game, if it amused him.

''I didn't even know there *was* another son,''
admitted the oldest reporter, and looked round the
assembled and now oddly quiet company for confirmation. Heads nodded and voices murmured; there
was another son.

''Oh, yes, he exists, all right,'' Hugh said
sombrely, handing along the refilled pint-pot to Dave,
and passing a pound note back to Nobbie at the bar.
He made a brief, impressive pause, and the interested
onlookers obligingly provided him with absolute
silence, which he knew exactly when to break. ''*I've*

seen him!'' he said in a sepulchral whisper; and that was all.

In the electric hush that followed, Nobbie's sense of mischief got the better of her. She looked round the circle of intense faces, the natives and the strangers, and then deliberately smacked down a handful of silver and coppers on the bar.

"Your change, Mr. Macsen-Martel!"

The awful pause felt like a year, but was actually no more than a couple of seconds. Then, with exquisite tact, everyone not directly involved turned, formed new and casual groups, and began to talk about the weather and football. It was done, and seen to be done, not in order to bury the shock for ever, but merely to keep it on ice while the victims were given a chance to slip away, so that their discomfiture could be properly and privately enjoyed by those who belonged here. And slip away they did, scarlet and speechless and hideously embarrassed. The youngest one, without so much as a word to anyone, simply picked up his coat and slunk out, the other two made a pitiful attempt to carry it off with forced smiles and a sudden pretence that they had just noticed how late it was. The big photographer, who had said least and committed himself least, took his time about withdrawing, and looked round the room defiantly before he went. In particular he looked with fixed interest at Hugh, who had not moved a muscle or said a word to ease the situation.

"You know, I *thought* you looked a bit like the old lady."

It was an artificial exit line, and Hugh could quite well have said: "Liar!" Instead, and just as devastatingly, he said: "God forbid!" which shook the photographer considerably more.

"Oh, I don't know," he said uneasily. "Fine, straight old lady for her age. Must be seventy, I suppose?'' His eye flickered round the bar once again. "Very interesting evening! And a very interesting door!'' he added with recovered assurance, and walked out with a curious private smile on his face.

The inhabitants stirred, sighed, cautiously stretched, expanding to fill the quitted space.

"Did you *have* to do that?'' Hugh asked Nobbie reproachfully.

"Did *you* have to?'' murmured Dinah resignedly.

"Coming to something,'' marvelled Willie the Twig, "when those boys get hypersensitive.''

Saul put back his teeth, and ordered one of Ellie Crouch's pork pies. And Nobbie, patting her blonde kiss-curl into place, said complacently: "I reckon I won, anyhow. And *they* won't be back in a hurry.'' For so far from inviting alien custom, "The Sitting Duck'' was constantly compelled to protect its limited supplies of home-brewed in the interests of its regulars.

Nevertheless, within ten days one of the strangers did come back. And this time to stay.

CHAPTER 2

THE PHOTOGRAPHER from Birmingham reappeared in Mottisham unexpectedly on a Tuesday morning of mid-October, shortly before noon. It was the first foggy day of the autumn, in a month which tended to be productive of thick mists in the deep, river-threaded cleft of Middlehope; but it was not the low visibility that brought the stranger crawling into the forecourt of Cressett and Martel at approximately fifteen miles an hour, and caused him to heave a sigh of relief at his safe arrival. Somewhere along the road from Comerbourne he had hit a stray stone, probably shed from a lorry, and his steering had begun to afflict him at the most inconvenient moments with a terrifying judder. He had no intention of driving a car with that sort of handicap any farther than he had to on a foggy day, and Dave's was the first garage at the Comerbourne side of the village. The driver clambered out thankfully, and Dave came out from the workshop to serve him.

He recognised the shock-head of straw-coloured hair and the slightly racy clothes at once. "Oh, hullo, back again? What's the trouble?"

The photographer was willing to talk. His name was Gerry Bracewell, he lived in Edgbaston—he produced a business card to prove it—and he had just driven over to take one more look at that church door, and maybe the house it came from, too. Very interesting thing, that, he said with a sly, self-satisfied smile. And now his steering had practically packed it in on him, and could Dave do anything about it by this evening? Or tomorrow morning, if necessary, he might be staying overnight in any case.

"Taking photographs in this weather?" Dave couldn't refrain from asking him casually.

Bracewell grinned. He had an amiable, cocky, knowing smile that belonged to the city. "Haven't even brought a camera along this time. No, just interested. You never know where there may be a story lurking, do you? Pictures I can get later if there's anything in it." He prowled the yard while Dave looked at the sick Morris, and for the first time his eye fell upon the two names above the entrance. "*Martel*? Is that the same one?"

"It's all right," said Dave drily from the driving-seat, "he's gone into Comerbourne with a respray job. Yes, it's the same one. He's my partner."

"One of the Macsen-Martels? That lot that gave the door back to the church?"

"The one that got away," said Dave. "He's been working here with me nearly four years. It's what he likes doing, and what he's good at."

"Well, bully for him! A bit of a card, isn't he?"

"That leg-pull in the 'Duck'? They like their fun. I wouldn't take too much notice, if I were you."

Bracewell came closer. "He fall out with his folks, or something? I mean, it's a bit unusual to find somebody like him cutting loose like this and working with his hands, isn't it?"

"Not particularly. Inevitable, I should say. Feudal families are living in changed circumstances these days. All the land that went with the house is gone long ago, there never was much money. Robert works in an office, Hugh works here. They have to live."

Not a talkative chap, Bracewell thought. Dave had told him nothing he couldn't have got from anyone in the village. "This National Trust business. You think they'll take the place on?"

"I think they will. It's more or less agreed, I believe." He himself did not think all that highly of the Abbey as an architectural monument; just a stark grey stone house with a single vast expanse of roof, and blunt, massive chimneys; but apparently there were those who did. Parts of it dated from Edward the Fourth, so they said, notably the vaulted cellars, but Dave was as little impressed by mere age as was Hugh himself. But the urgent fact was that there was no money to maintain the property, the roof, according to Hugh, leaked in half a dozen places, and something had to be done about it quickly. Either sell it—which would probably mean selling it for demolition and redevelopment—or else get the National Trust to take it over, help to maintain it, and permit the former owners to continue in residence on condition that they showed it perhaps once a week. Well, that was about as good a deal as Robert was likely to get.

"But what's the door got to do with it? Why move a door?" Bracewell's tone had sunk to a confidential level. "Won't the National Trust people object, anyhow?"

"Not if it didn't belong there, why should they? They'll want to take over something as authentic as possible." He slid out of the car again, and wiped his hands. "All right, leave her with me, and I'll see what I can do. I don't think it's so bad. I'll try and have it ready for you this evening, barring emergencies."

"Fine! How late are you on the job?"

"Six, officially, but I'll be here." He nodded towards the house, solid and stolid in pleasant, mottled brick beyond the yard and the pumps.

"Right, but if I'm not here before six, I'll probably be staying over, so don't wait around for me. If I don't show tonight, I'll be in pretty early tomorrow.

O.K.?'' He fished a plump and elderly briefcase out of the back of the Morris, and departed with a confident and springy step towards the village.

Dave Cressett had run the garage for twelve years, ever since his father's early death. He was thirty-four now, and a highly responsible, taciturn and resolute thirty-four into the bargain, having assumed mature cares early. His stature was small, his manner neat, unobtrusive and workmanlike, and his appearance nondescript, with a set of pleasant, good-natured features that seemed to be made up of oddments until he smiled, when everything fell beautifully into place. He didn't smile too often, because he was by inclination a serious soul; but it was worth waiting for. Not a firework display like Hugh's dazzling laughter, which he shed so prodigally all around him, but the comforting and dependable radiance of a good fire. Everything about him was equally reliable; which was why business had prospered for Cressett and Martel. Hugh tuned and raced the firm's cars, with dash and success, but it was on Dave that the clients depended.

Dave had known Hugh since school days, though there were five years between them. He had known Robert, too, for he was within a year of Robert's age; but nobody had ever really known Robert, sunk as he had been beneath the weight of being the heir, even if there was precious little to inherit, and threatened to be progressively less, and ultimately nothing at all, barring a monstrous minus of debts, if his father lived much longer. Hugh was different. Hugh was carefree, did what he liked and asked afterwards, mixed with whatever company he pleased and never asked at all, got his face dirty and his nails broken playing around with motors when he should have been accumulating O and A levels, and didn't give a damn for his Norman blood or his aristocratic status. In fact, he was so like his delightful, unpredictable,

eighteenth-century anachronism of a father that there
was no mistaking the implications. They represented,
between them, a late burst of demoniac energy in a
line practically burned out. You had only to look at
the mother—seven years older than her husband, and
his first-cousin; they always interbred—and the elder
brother to see what had happened to the race, long
since bled into debility, overtaken and left standing
by history. Tenacious stock, time had shown that; but
exhausted at last. Somebody had to break out, marry
fresh blood, get fresh heirs and plunge into fresh
activities. The ghost of the name would take some
laying, but Hugh already stood clear of it, neutral as a
clinical observer from outer space. After all, the crude
reality was that the name meant nothing now; the
doctor and the hotel-keeper ranked higher in impor-
tance than the attenuated representatives of past
glory, and the vigorous incomers from the towns far
higher. Hugh was the one who took the realities as
they came, and did not feel his powers and possibilities in any way limited.

For Dave all these considerations were very
relevant indeed, because Hugh had worked himself
into a partnership nearly four years ago, and the tacit
understanding between him and Dinah had been
growing and proliferating ever since. It wasn't even a
question of waiting for a concrete proposal; people
like Dinah and Hugh didn't function in that way,
they simply grew together without words, and some
day, still without words and without question, got
married. If Dave knew his sister and his partner, that
day was creeping up on them fast.

As far as Dave could see, it wasn't going to have
much to do with him, when it came to the point.
Dinah was ten years his junior, and he had had to be
father and mother to her, as well as brother, but she
was twenty-four years old now, and a remarkably self-

sufficient young woman, who ran the house, did the firm's books and occasionally relieved Jenny Pelsall in the office, with apparent ease. She had all the equipment she needed, a heart, a head, a chin and a backbone. She was a pocket edition, like her brother, but good stuff lies in little compass. He wasn't worried about Dinah, she'd find her own way, and if she chose Hugh, she wouldn't be choosing him just for a blinding smile and a light hand on a gear-lever.

He'd got her as far as consenting to go and spend this particular evening with his people at the Abbey; the first formal encounter, this would be, but no amount of Norman blood—or blood of the princes of Powis, either, for that matter—could intimidate Dinah. And, as Hugh said, what the hell, we're not tied to the place, we don't have to stick around here if we don't want to. Admittedly it's a bit of an ordeal, Robert's pretty dreary, to say the least of it, and the old girl's virtually petrified in her devotion to her sacred line. But don't let it throw you, we don't have to see much of them when we're married. And Dinah had said thoughtfully that she supposed they had to get it over sooner or later. Just so long, she had said, as you bring me home before I blow my top. We may not have to live in the same village afterwards, but we do have to live in the same world. And he had promised gaily, all the more readily because bringing Dinah home gave him the best excuse possible for not sleeping overnight at the Abbey. He retained his room there to please his mother, and slept in it when he had to, but he much preferred the free life in the flatlet they'd made for him over the workshop in the yard. Grooms, he said, ought to live above the stable.

Sometimes he sounded, sometimes he even looked, like his dead father, who had come head-over-heels off a horse at an impossible fence five winters ago, when the Middlehope hounds drew the shoulder of Callow, the everyone else diverged cravenly towards the gate. He had fallen on his head and shoulders and broken his neck, and there went the last survivor of the eighteenth century in these borders, trailing his comet's-tail of heroic stories, amorous, bibulous and equestrian. For years he'd arrived and departed as unpredictably as hurricane weather, vanishing whenever he got too far into debt or into difficulties, or too many local girls were in full cry after him with paternity suits, reappearing after his wife and son had got things under control again, and always finding a warm welcome waiting. Hugh had his fierce good looks and sudden disarming moods of sweetness and hilarity; but Hugh didn't run after women or plunge head-down into debt. He doted on cars, raced them, doctored them, made respectable money out of them. And Dinah was his only girl.

The fog thickened a little again towards evening, and Hugh was late getting back from Comerbourne. The resprayed car had to be delivered to one of the new houses on the other side of the village, which meant a ten-minute walk back from there; and Dinah was ready and waiting some time before the back door crashed open in the usual head-long style, to indicate that the junior partner was home. He came in wreathed in chilly mist and glowing apologies, six feet of tightly strung nervous energy even at the end of the working day.

Dinah rose and picked up her coat. She was wearing a plain, long-sleeved shift in a delirious orange-and-olive print, that stopped short five inches above her knees.

"You'll shake the old lady rigid," Dave observed, eyeing her impartially.

"From all accounts she already is rigid, anyhow. Begin as you mean to go on, I say. After all, she knows her darling boy, she wouldn't expect him to come around with a nun.''

Hugh took the wheel as of right. It was rare for him to consent to be a passenger. She thought his touch a little edgy, though as assured as ever. Very revealing, that, Dinah considered. It looked as if he was a little more worked up about this confrontation than he pretended, and certainly more than she was.

''You won't like it,'' he said, confirming her speculations as to his state of mind. It was as near an apology for his family as he was ever likely to get.

''You never know, I might. I'm contra-suggestible. I might even like your folks, it has been known to happen in these cases.''

He gave a hollow laugh. ''That'll be the day! Still, we needn't even stay within range, when we're married. We could go abroad, if you'd like it. I bet you and I could do well in Canada. Did you ever think about it?—clearing out and starting fresh somewhere else?''

''No,'' said Dinah comfortably, ''I never did. And you never did, either, until tonight. Anyhow, who said we were going to be married? Relax, boy, it won't be that bad!''

He relaxed a little. They were feeling their way steadily along the misty green lane behind the hotel, watching for the open gate that led into the Abbey drive. The entrance was narrow and dark, shrouded in trees. Nothing was left of the monastic buildings that had once stretched clean across the centre of the present village, except the lumpy bases of walls just breaking the ground in two places in the shrubberies. Only the abbot's lodging remained. They saw the long level of the high roof faintly against a clearing sky, the thick column of the chimneys. Only two lighted windows broke the murky dimness. The house looked dank, dilapidated and cold.

"Look, Dinah, once we're installed, I'll take
Robert away for a bit—don't you think?—and let you
get down to it in earnest with Mother. You won't
mind, will you? We won't stay away long. But I'm
betting on it that once you've broken the ice she'll be
eating out of your hand." He rolled the car to a halt
before the crumbling porch, and turned and gave her
a slightly strained smile. "After all, that's the way
you affected *me*, isn't it?"

"Straight in at the deep end!" mused Dinah. He
was evidently more disturbed by the whole thing than
she had guessed. "All right, kill or cure. Maybe we'll
end up in Canada, after all."

The door opened ponderously but silently on a
long, flagged hall, none too adequately lit, that
stretched clean through the house and ended at a
broad Gothic window. Dinah's alert eye noted worn
mats, bare panelling, a vast oaken staircase, the stone
newels of what must be the steps down to the cellar,
just to the left of the terminal window, and a narrow
little lobby bearing away to the right, and ending in a
garden door. The coats that hung in the lobby were so
old and so frequently dry-cleaned that they had out-
lived all their original quality and cut, and most of
their colour. Even if there had been nothing else to
betray their age, the length of the nearest, a woman's
classic camel coat, would have been enough. Mrs.
Macsen-Martel was tall, but even on her this skirt
would practically reach the ankle. Everything had
been good in its day; and for everything within sight
its day was long over.

Someone had heard them come. A door on the
right, beyond the stairs, opened, and Robert came
out to greet them.

It was the first time Dinah had had the opportunity
to study him at such close quarters, and she gazed at
him with candid interest, looking for some resem-

blance to Hugh. The long, lightweight bones were the same, the hollowed cheeks, even the deep setting of the eyes, but in place of Hugh's vivid colouring and mobility, this one was neutral-tinted and hesitant, almost deprecating, of movement. A profound, almost a fastidious reserve dominated everything in his face, the brown eyes that were at such pains to avoid staring at her, the long, level mouth that opened stiffly to welcome her.

"Miss Cressett, I'm so glad you could come. Let me take your coat." But he moved too slowly, and Hugh had already taken it. "Do come in, my mother's looking forward to meeting you." She was surprised but thankful that he didn't say: "We've heard so much about you from Hugh." Maybe he was leaving that for the old lady. Someone was certainly due to say it before the evening was over.

Hugh took her possessively by the elbow, and steered her into the drawing-room. Large, lofty, chilly, with a vast fireplace and a very modest fire in the distant wall, and a few good but threadbare rugs deployed artfully to make the maximum impression of comfort where there was little that was comfortable. A great deal of splendid but sombre furniture—there was money there, at any rate, if they cared to realise it —and one superb, high-backed, erect chair placed near the fire and facing the door, with the old woman enthroned in it. A tableau especially for Dinah's benefit; she had to walk approximately twenty-five feet across the bare centre of the room to reach her hostess, with the faded, lofty-lidded eyes watching and appraising her every step of the way. All those exposed inches of smooth, slim thigh in honey-beige tights, the short, almost boyish cap of dark-brown hair, and greenish eye-shadow, the fashionable chunky shoes that Dave called her football boots . . . But if I'd worn a crinoline, she thought, watching the old woman's face every bit as narrowly as her own face was being watched, I should still have come as a shock.

Hugh did the only thing he could do to break the tension, and did it beautifully. He dropped Dinah's elbow and swooped ahead of her, shearing through the invisible cord that linked the two pairs of hostile female eyes; he stooped and kissed his mother's grey and fallen cheek, and warmed her face for a moment into genuine life.

"Hullo, Mother! Here's Dinah, I promised I'd bring her to see you, didn't I?" He reached for Dinah's other hand as his mother put up an emaciated claw and allowed her bony fingers to be clasped for a moment in Dinah's short-nailed, well-scrubbed, capable hand. It was like holding a dead bird, starved in the winter cold. Two rings, old-fashioned ones, but those were surely real rubies in them . . . and that long string of beads dangling into her lap to complete the elongated effect of every line of her body was neither of glass nor cultures, but pearls. Of course, she'd been from the branch of the family with some money left, until she married Robert senior, and he got his hands on most of it and sent it flying like skittles . . . I am a right *bitch*, thought Dinah, shocked behind her dutiful smile. I should blame her for walking round me with her hackles up, what else do I deserve? And penitence gave her a surge of positive benevolence. She wondered if she dared kiss . . . No, there was no invitation being signalled. On the contrary, the released hand was flexing inflexible fingers delicately under the edge of the dun-coloured lace stole, as if the clasp had bruised them.

"So kind of you to give up an evening to a dull old woman like me, Miss Cressett. Do sit down . . . " She gestured vaguely towards a velvet hassock that would have installed Dinah at her feet, but Hugh was

splendidly blind, and whisked up a comfortable
leather chair close to his mother's, to establish them
as equals. Dinah gave him a lightning glance that
would have liked to turn into a wink, and sat down
with as little display of leg as she could manage.
Appeasement was not in her nature, but whenever
she looked at poor Hugh she had pacific thoughts.

"Perhaps you would care for a glass of something?
I don't drink myself, but perhaps a sherry . . . ?"

"I brought a case of Traminer," said Hugh unexpectedly, "we can try it with dinner if it suits. I was
in town, and had to wait all day for my job, so I went
shopping, and got hold of a real bargain. It's
Jugoslav, but it's as good as most that comes out of
Alsace. I know, I've tried it! Come and help me fetch
it in, Rob, it's in the boot of the car."

If it really was, Dinah thought with deep interest,
then he'd popped it in there before he even came into
the house. Indeed he must have dropped it off inside
the yard before he delivered the respray job across in
Greenfields, and installed it ready for delivery on his
return. Her attention was caught in a new and grave
way. If Hugh was as keyed up as all that, scheming
with cases of wine and worrying about the impression
she was going to make on his mother (not to mention
the impression his mother was probably going to
make on her!) then there was really nothing else for it,
he *must* be in love. And she thought, calmed, assuaged
and flattered, having someone like Hugh that much in
love is a good reason for being in love with him. She
had always wondered. Now she began to feel certain.

Robert—how silent he was, did he never have
anything to say in this household?—brought her a
glass of sherry. She looked up in his face as she
accepted it; such a middle-aged face, and he was only
thirty-five, after all. Bleached, brownish hair, straight
as pen-feathers, cropped close; not a badly-shaped

head at all, but so defeated, so inanimate. Tired eyes, darker brown, so withdrawn that there was no knowing whether they were indifferent to her, or simply burdened past caring. He almost never spoke, but his voice was low, pleasantly pitched and sad; yet distantly disapproving, too. He was not on her side. Beware of the gentle people who do not rant, but nevertheless are not amenable to anyone's wiles. In his way he was as rigid as his mother.

And that, as Dinah discovered when they were left alone together, was pretty rigid. The air seemed to clarify as soon as the men were out of the way. Like a sudden change of wind sweeping the mist from a battlefield.

"Hugh has told me so much about you, Miss Cressett." (She'd known that was coming, sooner or later! It meant: Be careful, I'm warned, I'm on the alert!) "He thinks very highly of you. Do tell me something about yourself, my dear, I don't think I'm acquainted with your family. What was your father?'

"He owned the same garage we run now. *His* father was a very early motorist in these parts, a pioneer, and Father followed in his footsteps. And so has my brother David—Hugh's partner . . . "

"Ah, yes, of course, I know from Hugh that your brother is in trade." It sounded like a category, the way she said it, and probably it was. "And where were you at school, Miss Cressett?''

Dinah told her, bluntly: the village primary, then the secondary modern at Abbot's Bale. "I wasn't an academic type. Mine are mostly manual skills. I keep house. Quite well, I believe. At least no one complains."

"I'm quite sure you are good at everything you attempt. One feels so out of date these days." Her long fingers strayed languidly among her pearls. The long, straight lines of brow, nose and chin, in profile,

looked like a caricature of Edith Sitwell. The grey
hair, drawn closely back into that great knot on her
nape, weighed down her whole head and shoulders
into an effete arc the moment she relaxed her guard.
"In my day gels were educated to such different ends.
We had not to reckon with trade, of course . . . This
has become such a commercial world, has it not?"
She leaned back with a sigh, and all the oblique grey
planes of her face, and shoulders, and fleshless bust
slithered downwards into a pyramid of discouragement and decay. "The name Cressett is old . . . are
you connected with the Northamptonshire Cressetts,
by any chance?"

"I doubt it," said Dinah cheerfully. "But I don't
suppose there's anyone in my family who can trace
his ancestors back more than three generations, four
at the most, so of course we could be. As far as I
know, we're Middlehope stock from way back."

The old lady closed her eyes for a fraction of a
second, perhaps praying for strength. The catechism
went on steadily: What were your mother's family?
What are your interests? Are you fond of music? You
play of course? (Naturally a lady plays the piano,
however badly.)

Thank God, they were coming back. There went
the outer door, hollowly closing, and in a moment
more the two brothers came rather quietly, rather
warily, into the room. At least the Traminer was real
enough, Hugh had a bottle in one hand and a
corkscrew in the other. They bore themselves, Dinah
thought, a little stiffly, as if there was some related
awkwardness even between them. They had so little
in common that with all the goodwill in the world
communication might well be an effort for both.

"Dinner's ready," Robert said. "Will you come,
Mother?"

Over dinner it was much easier, though the table in

the large, chilly room, even when reduced to its minimum proportions, was too big for comfortable conversation between four people. But at least there *were* four of them, and every time the catechism showed signs of being resumed Dinah could answer monosyllabically, and then address some quick remark to one of the men, even if Hugh did not anticipate her need, as he frequently did. She had felt a certain amount of childish curiosity about the meal itself, and the manner of its presentation. Would the old lady have cooked it herself? Not much doubt that she could, that was one of the things gels in her day had been expected to master. But in all probability on this occasion the cooking had been done by the same local help who brought in the dishes. Plain, good English cottage cooking, nothing elaborate and nothing expensive. And having installed the joint and vegetables on the sideboard—the pudding being cold—the cook said good night and departed, plainly for home. It was Robert who served everything, silently, unobtrusively and attentively. Once there had been some four or five servants living in at the Abbey; now there was Robert, and Robert was everything. Dinah tried to imagine Hugh shouldering this load, tamed into this grey tameness, and the picture was so absurd as to be almost indecent.

Mrs. Macsen-Martel could even say: "I'm so glad you find the veal to your liking, Miss Cressett," in such a way as to make Dinah feel that she had been eating like a hungry wolf. And indeed she was hungry; emotional excitement always had that effect on her.

"It's really excellent," she said defensively, and turned on Robert with the first thing that entered her head. After all, that celebrated door was the chief event of the past week in Mottisham, what could be more natural than to show curiosity about it?

"I've been dying to ask you about that door you gave back to the church. It's almost the only thing—I mean apart from bits of the stone fabric—that's left from the Gothic church, isn't it? The rebuilders in the last century finished off almost everything else that survived. So it's really very important, being local work, too. With a long history like that, it must have some legends attached to it, hasn't it?"

Robert seemed to emerge with a spasmodic effort from the glum abstraction into which he sank between his bouts of hospitable assiduity. She saw his long bones convulsed for an instant as he hauled himself back into awareness of her.

"They might be anything but true," he said with evident reluctance. "They do exist, yes, but only as legends."

"My dear," murmured the old lady, her thin brows elevated into her dust-coloured hair. "The cellar door? Legends? I've never heard that it was anything more than a *door*. What legends?"

"There isn't any documentary evidence, how could there be?" Robert sounded tired, but as always, obliging. "The abbey library was quite simply bundled out and burned, so we shall never know whether there were any written records. Probably not, the abbey had a blameless reputation up to the fifteenth century, its decline was part of the general rot that was partly responsible for the Dissolution—or at least for the ease and general consent with which it was carried out. And what was in the chronicles was usually a hundred years past—by the end there weren't any chroniclers. I doubt if the last four could write English, much less Latin."

"You mean it's true," asked Dinah, astonished, "that there were only four brothers left here at the end, and they weren't any model of holiness?"

"They were anything but. And for that there *is*

good evidence. You know something about the end of the abbey, then?''

''I didn't,'' she admitted honestly, ''except that they were talking about it in 'The Sitting Duck' on Sunday night.''

''They?''

'Saul Trimble,'' Hugh supplied with a reminiscent grin. ''And believe me, he shouldn't be underestimated. The essence of his nonsense is that about sixty per cent of it at least is good sense. It makes it more baffling. Even sceptics make inquiries, and get converted.''

''Quite a lot of the monastic houses had degenerated badly by that time,'' Robert said, ''especially the more remote ones that were a law to themselves. And ours was pretty remote. This tale about the church door belongs towards the end. They say one of the brothers—there must have been more than four then —had made the classic pact with the devil, signing away his soul in return for diabolical help in this world, especially at raising spirits, and then tried to back out of the bargain at the crucial hour by taking refuge in the church. But wherever he tried to enter, the doors remained barred against him. In his despair he fell on his knees in the south porch and clutched at the sanctuary knocker, as the best he could do, but the cold iron burned his hand as if it had been red-hot, and forced him to loose his hold. And the devil took him.'' Robert's quiet voice quivered momentarily. Such a pale, still face . . . Dinah shivered, watching him. She had never really noticed him before, only recorded externals, measuring a potential enemy. ''Not physically, however. According to the story, the monks came down for Prime, and found his body huddled at the foot of the door, stone dead. No marks on him, not even a burned hand.''

''How very odd,'' said the old lady with detached

disapproval, "that I never remember hearing this nonsense before! And what nonsense it is! Just a perfectly ordinary door!"

"I quite agree," admitted Robert. "Most such stories are nonsense, but people go on telling them. The door has always been credited—or discredited—with being haunted, but I can't say we ever had any odd experiences with it here, or noticed anything queer about it. I don't know—maybe we're just inured, because we lived with all these things so intimately and so long. The time might come when one took even ghosts for granted, and failed to see them . . ."

Dinah shuddered and shook herself. Perhaps, she thought, even that could happen, when you belong only to the past; not even to the present, much less the future. And she thought, well, yes, there's always Canada—or Australia, where you have to be real or people fail to see *you*!

She thought of the antique iron beast, playfully proffering his twisted ring of hope, and grinning as it burned the desperate hand that reached for it. For the rest of the evening—mercifully it was short, old people retire early—she could not get it out of her head. She was grateful to Hugh for his delicacy and affection when he broke up the coffee-party in the drawing-room—Robert had made the coffee, of course!—and took her tenderly home through the thinning fog, at a slow speed which permitted him to keep an arm about her all the way. He was warm, quiet and bracing. She was practically sure that she loved him.

Dave was brewing tea in the kitchen when she came in from the yard, with Hugh's kiss still warm and confident on her lips, and her backward glance still illuminated by the light from Hugh's flat over the

stable. He hadn't drawn the curtains, and he had just
hauled off his shirt and plunged across the bedroom
towards the shower-room beyond. Then the light
went out, and the October night swallowed him.
Good night, Hugh!

"That Brummagem bloke didn't come in for his
car," Dave said. She hardly heard him, she was so far
away. "He must be staying overnight. He said he
might. Wonder what on earth he expected to find
worth his while in these parts?"

"Ghosts, hobgoblins, pacts, devils . . . who
knows?' said Dinah, yawning. "Witchcraft and such
is *news* these days, didn't you know?"

"How did it go?" asked Dave curiously.

"Oh, not so bad! They're dead," she said simply,
"but never mind, Hugh's alive." She wandered to
bed, hazy with Traminer. Dave watched her go,
reassured. As for Bracewell, he'd be in early in the
morning, just as he'd said.

But early is a relative term, and freelance photographers, perhaps, keep different hours from office
workers, garage proprietors and such slaves of the
clock. The Brummagem bloke had still not put in an
appearance to claim his repaired Morris when Dave
drove the vicar's third-hand Cortina back to the
vicarage, on its new tyres at just after nine o'clock, as
promised. His nearest way back to the garage was
through the churchyard. Thus it was Dave who
happened to be the first person to pass close by the
south porch on this misty Wednesday morning, and
casting the native's natural side-glance towards the
legendary door within, register the startling
apparition of size ten shoe-soles jutting into the dawn.

There was a man inside the shoes. The dim light
under the trees drew in outline long, trousered legs in
flannel grey, the hem of a short car coat, bulky

shoulders under brown gaberdine, straw-coloured hair spilled on the flagstones from a lolling head that was not quite the right shape.

Dave advanced by inches, chilled and yet irresistibly drawn. He saw an extended arm, fingers and palm flattened against the foot of the closed door. He stepped over the sprawled legs, and peered at the motionless face. The eyes were open, glazed and bright, glaring at the shut door, straining after the calm within. The jaw had dropped, as if parted upon a desperate cry for help.

The photographer from Birmingham, who had sensed a story here in the barbarian territory of Middlehope, and staked his freelance reputation upon cornering the scoop, was never going to file his story after all. He was dead and cold at the foot of the sanctuary door.

CHAPTER 3

DAVE STARTED back for the vicarage at a run. The nearest telephone was there, and the vicar had to know, in any case, and was by far the most suitable person to stand guard over the scene until the police arrived. The one thing everyone knows about the scene of a crime—especially a murder—is that nothing must be moved or touched until the whole circus has had its way. That this was a crime was not in doubt for a moment. And not merely a murderous assault, but a murder. The large, jagged stone that lay in the middle of the flagged path, ominously stained, had not fallen out of the trees; there was a gap among the whitened stones fringing the grass, to show where someone had plucked it from, and there was the dark, muddied red hollow in the photographer's skull to show what the same someone had done with it. There was no misting of breath on metal when Dave held his silver lighter against the open lips, the hand he touched gingerly was marble-cold. It never entered his head to think of a doctor. Doctors weren't going to do anything for this poor devil from now on, except haggle over the time and the exact cause of his death.

The Reverend Andrew, a realistic soul, accepted what he was told without demanding that it be repeated. When he said something he meant it, and not being lavish or fluent with words, he expected to have the few he did use taken as gospel. Moreover, he recognised a like directness in Dave. He waved him at once to the telephone, and galloped off towards the churchyard, to mount guard over the body that must have lain unguarded all night. And Dave called, not headquarters at Comerbourne, as the vicar would probably have done, but Sergeant Moon, up the valley at Abbot's Bale. The moment the outside world laid an encroaching hand on the property, privacy or peace of mind of Middlehope, the whole valley closed its ranks.

"Stand by, and we'll be down there in a quarter of an hour," said Sergeant Moon. "Don't leave him alone, but don't let anyone touch anything."

"No, that's taken care of—the vicar's keeping an eye on him."

And Dave went to join him. The Reverend Andrew was examining everything in the south porch with appalled but fascinated eyes, as closely as he could without disturbing anything. He wasn't a native, and he was young enough and innocent enough to find life in Middlehope a little wanting in action—being excluded by his office from about nine-tenths of what action there really was. He would have been horrified if it had so much as entered his mind that he could be glad of a murder; but here was one on his doorstep whether he wanted it or not, and it was impossible not to feel a decided curiosity, and even a certain distinctly pleasurable excitement.

"Desecrated!" he said, looking over his shoulder at Dave from his precious door. "This means we shall have to get it reconsecrated all over again."

"A pity we can't just do the same for him," Dave said drily. He couldn't take his eyes from the mis-shapen head and the jagged stone with its stained edges. He thought of fragments of hair and skin adhering, to make the manner of the assault certain, and of fingerprints to identify the hand that had held the weapon. But no, not from that stone, not a hope!

It was a bright, whitish lump, full of mica crystals, without a smooth surface anywhere on it. More likely, perhaps, to have abraded the attacker's fingertips when he struck with it, and collected some sample of skin or blood tissue that might lead to him by another way. There was a police forensic laboratory in Birmingham; the full treatment would be available within a couple of hours at the most.

The thought was at once reassuring and chilling, as though the valley had already been invaded by the apparatus of unlawful death, as indeed it had from the moment the stone was plucked out of the grass. No going back now. Dave had never felt himself so much a native. He also felt, to tell the truth, a little sick, but no one looking at his dour, quiet face would have realised it.

If he had ever entertained any idea that the law moved slowly and sleepily in these parts, he was soon disabused of it. Sergeant Moon and one of his constables came rattling down the valley from Abbot's Bale in the sergeant's old Ford within thirteen minutes, slipped the car inside the vicarage drive, and arrived without alerting the village. The relief and security Dave felt at the very sight of the big sergeant was illuminating; after all, he was only Middlehope at all by marriage, but of his membership in the islanded community here there could no longer be any doubt. He might have been there since before Eliseg's grandson set up the memorial pillar to him, over in Wales. He even walked and talked like a Middlehope man. Easy to see why he never wanted to move away, not even for promotion. What did he want with promotion, when he was already, after his fashion, a minor prince?

"Ah," said the sergeant, considering the body of the photographer from Birmingham with the same gravity and calm with which he daily summed up the weather prospects at the edge of winter, and estimated his commitment in case of isolation. "Stranger. Didn't I see him last Sunday? With a camera?" It was not really a question, unless to himself, and already provided with its answer. Dave said nothing, not yet. When the sergeant wanted anything from him, he'd ask for it.

"You found him, Dave? Statements come later, now just tell me." Sergeant Moon knew every soul who belonged in his domain, and could call them all by their first names.

Dave told him, slowly and accurately, with times. He knew when he'd left home, he knew how long it took to drive a car round into the vicarage garage and walk back here. 'I know who he is —or at least I know who he said he was. He brought his car in to our place yesterday morning with damaged steering, and gave me his card. He said he might stay overnight. I had the car ready last night, but I didn't think anything when he didn't come for it, after what he'd said. His name's Bracewell. And you're right, he was here on Sunday covering the service. He was in 'The Sitting Duck' that evening. That's all I know about him. Except that he was interested in that door—more than most, I mean. As if he thought he was on to something special about it, and thought he might get a good story out of it. I don't know how, he didn't say."

For Dave it was quite a speech. The sergeant patted his shoulder vaguely, and digested, with no vagueness at all, what he had told him. The Reverend Andrew hovered, with nothing to do but confirm the circumstances that had brought him there.

And then, within three quarters of an hour of the discovery of the body, the whole apparatus suddenly went into top gear. The succession of events was bewildering. First came the valley police doctor, hurtling in preoccupied and surly to kneel beside the dead man, touch him delicately, probe half-heartedly for a temperature (the body was fully clothed for an autumn night) and think better of it. Let the pathologist worry about the precise time of death—not that it would be very precise in the circumstances!— when he got here from Comerbourne. The doctor confirmed the indisputable fact of death, cast one significant glance at the all too obvious matter now darkening and drying on the stone, and withdrew in businesslike fashion to his practice. He had a lot of patients waiting and a lot of territory to cover afterwards, and the sergeant had caught him just at the opening of his surgery.

Hard on his heels came a police van from Comerbourne with the photography team, and a car containing a detective constable as driver, one detective sergeant, Chief Inspector George Felse, and Dr. Reece Goodwin, the hospital pathologist who bore the blessing of the Home Office in these parts. Detective Superintendent Duckett, the head of the county C.I.D., had been in his car somewhere on the way to consult his Chief Constable about something quite different—a matter of certain local bank frauds —when Moon's call came through, and thus fate dropped the case into George's hands from its inception. Duckett might well be along later, when the message reached him. Moon, to be truthful, rather hoped not; he got on better with George.

"I shouldn't have said it," owned George resignedly. 'Soon found a way to fetch me back, didn't you?" He looked the scene over for a moment in silence, and arrived at the vicar and Dave, still patiently in attendance.

"Dave Cressett here found him," said Moon practically. "He's a busy man, with a garage and filling station to look after, and not two minutes away when wanted. Now if the vicar here could loan us a room as office, that would be the most convenient arrangement for everybody.''

The Reverend Andrew, appalled and delighted, was willing to make over half of his monstrous vicarage to them if required, and said so. Nothing half as interesting as this had happened to him since he came to Mottisham, and the prospect of a front seat on the investigation was dreadfully attractive.

"All right, Jack, you get a preliminary statement from Mr. Cressett, and I'll see him later on."

Dave looked back curiously as he was ushered, with Sergeant Moon, back into the vicarage gates, crossing the main road, where now the infallible grape-vine had already assembled a small and watchful audience, conversing in pregnant whispers. The team of photographers circled and aimed and manoeuvred round the porch, focusing the body, the weapon, the outflung hand and broken head. Dr. Goodwin, a round, bounding, energetic man who appeared fifty and was actually pushing sixty-five, was on his knees beside the corpse. And one more car was just arriving, and decanting the forensic scientist from the laboratory in Birmingham, last of the team to put in an appearance.

Suddenly the south porch of St. Eata's was a seething hive of industry, and there were some eight or nine people clustered like bees in swarm round the indifferent body of Gerry Bracewell.

Before eleven o'clock they had lifted the body carefully into an outspread polythene sheet, retrieved the open briefcase from under it, and packed the deceased into a plastic shell, which was promptly whisked away under Dr. Goodwin's supervision to the hospital mortuary in Comerbourne. It was inconveniently far from the scene, but that was unavoidable, there was no suitable place nearer. The relevant exhibits had vanished with the man from the forensic laboratory. The south porch looked empty and innocent again, and the imperturbably amiable iron beast chewed his twisted ring and grinned as before. In the vicarage George made hurried notes before following the body to the mortuary, and somewhere on the road to Birmingham his sergeant fretted at a succession of red traffic lights, on his way to break the news to Mrs. Roberta Bracewell, and bring her to identify her husband's body. It was a job that mustn't be put off, but on the other hand couldn't be indecently rushed. George reckoned he had plenty of time to call at Dave Cressett's garage, and still be at the mortuary before the post mortem could begin.

The Morris was four years old, none too well maintained, and had accumulated the usual hotchpotch of appurtenances official and unofficial, assortment of cleaning rags, old tools, paper tissues, folding red triangle for travel abroad, one left glove, a man's knitted scarf, a crumpled packet of cigarettes, a box of first-aid dressings and a dismembered morning paper, but nothing at all suggestive or interesting. It stood waiting in the rear part of the yard, beyond the workshop.

"You'll probably want to take it away," said Dave, watching the chief inspector's face attentively. A thin, dark, self-contained, mildly humorous face. Moon liked him, and Moon's liking was a decided recommendation.

"I doubt it," said George, "seeing he left it here with you yesterday morning, and it's been here ever since. Keep it for a couple of days, and I'll get it looked over here on the spot. It's as private as anywhere. When we've finished with it I'll clear it for you, and you can hand it over to the widow. Or if you prefer, we'll do that for you.''

''I'd rather do it myself. He left it here for a job to be done, and I'd like to hand it back in good order to whoever owns it now. There's a widow, then?''

''Yes, he was married. No children, apparently. He took just his briefcase out of the back there when you left, you said? Nothing else?''

''No, nothing else. He said he might stay overnight, so I thought nothing of it when he didn't show up in the evening.'' He wanted to ask if Bracewell had indeed booked a room at the Martel Arms Hotel, but he wasn't on that kind of terms with the chief inspector. If it had been Sergeant Moon he would have asked whatever he wanted to know, and Moon would have told him as much as he thought he should be told. George was to be encountering the shadow of Sergeant Moon on every side in this valley, but it didn't matter. Moon was his man, and could pick up at leisure what was withheld from his chief.

A confidence might always be worth a confidence in return. ''He booked in all right,'' said George. ''He left his pyjamas and shaving kit there in the room. Nobody realised he wasn't in overnight, because up here—but I realise I'm telling a native the facts of life—nobody bothers to lock hotel rooms or hand in keys. They thought he was sleeping a bit late this morning, but he hadn't asked for a call, so they never even wondered until around nine o'clock.'' He turned briskly away from the car. ''Now if I could have one more word with Miss Cressett and your partner . . .''

Dinah and Hugh were in the kitchen together, and the shocked and wary glances they turned when they were interrupted, and the way their low-pitched and subdued voices died upon the air, spoke for them.

''Don't let me disturb you,'' George said. ''I just

wanted to make sure on one point. On your way back from the Abbey last night—that would be at about ten o'clock?''

"Just about ten past when we got here," said Hugh. "I looked at my watch after we said good night."

"So probably around ten when you came through the village. You'd touch only one side of the churchyard on that route, I know, but did you see anyone moving around at that hour? Anywhere in that stretch?''

They had not, and said so. "Except Joe Lyon, just making off across the lane to the fields, on his way home," added Hugh. "But I bet you'll find he'd left the bar of the 'Duck' a couple of minutes before. He always leaves just before ten, he's got a long way to go."

"Nobody else at all?''

"Not a soul. It was misty and miserable outside.''

"Yes, that's true, not an attractive night. Then there's nothing else you can add? Nothing that might be relevant in any way?''

"There's one thing that's just *too* relevant," said Dinah abruptly. She looked at Hugh for guidance, but he was gazing back at her with eyes wide in wondering inquiry. "But it isn't a matter of fact at all, and you'll think I'm crazy. If it wasn't for the—the resemblance . . . .''

"Tell me," George suggested, "and let me judge.''

"It's what Dave told us about how he was found, huddled up facing the door, and with his hand stretched out touching it—as if he'd been holding the knocker when he was struck, and just slid down the door as he fell. Last night Robert told us a story about that door. There's supposed to have been another queer death connected with it, centuries ago.''

Light had dawned on Hugh. "Oh, *that*! But that's just nonsense, it doesn't mean anything."

"It means there could be people who think of the door in that way, plenty of people. It could even mean that someone might try to reproduce what's supposed to have happened all that time ago—supposing he wanted to kill at all, that would be one way of creating a complete fog around the act, wouldn't it? Even if there's nothing at all in the superstition itself, it could be effective, couldn't it?"

"What is this story? The door's supposed to have killed someone before?" asked George.

"Not so much killed him as refused to save him." Dinah told the story, as nearly as she could remember them in the words Robert had used. "But Mrs. Macsen-Martel said how odd, she couldn't remember hearing that legend before."

"My mother hears only what she wants to hear," Hugh said indulgently, "and she hates all this superstitious mush. If she met a couple of ghostly monks pacing along the gallery, she'd walk straight through them and pretend they weren't there. There are plenty of odd stories, there always are about old houses. But none of us ever think about them at all unless we're prodded. Dinah did *ask* about the door."

She admitted it. "Yes, I began it. But isn't it queer that this man Bracewell should be killed just there— close to the door—touching it? Exactly the same!"

"Oh, come off it!" protested Hugh bracingly. "Any moment you'll be crediting it that the devil took this one, too!"

"*I* shan't," said Dinah, "but once the word gets round, half Middlehope *will*. Maybe that's what somebody *wants* to happen."

George made no comment, merely thanked her and took his leave. But as he drove down the valley towards Comerbourne and the unpleasant and

lengthy rendezvous at the mortuary, he could not help
feeling that Dinah might turn out to be a true
prophet. Much worse, the first whispers of words like
"devil", "witchcraft", "ghost", would bring the
representatives of the more sensational Sunday papers
converging on Middlehope like hounds in full cry.
Some fast and determined work was indicated, if they
were to escape that fate.

He went over the facts and possibilities with Sergeant
Moon, at something after ten o'clock that night, in
the room the Reverend Andrew had placed at their
disposal. George was just back from the post mortem,
a conference with his superintendent and his Chief
Constable, and a round of brief calls arising. Moon
had sat tight in Mottisham and pumped all his most
useful acquaintances in addition to all the relevant
witnesses. Both were tired, and George had still to
compose his first report, which was a matter for great
care, since the future charge of the case largely
depended upon it.

"That's it, then. We know his movements for most
of the day. Arrived in the village about a quarter to
twelve, noon, yesterday, and left his car at Cressett's
for repair, taking his briefcase with him. Had lunch at
the Martel Arms and asked about a room. Left there,
still carrying his briefcase, but having unloaded his
night things from it, about two. Was seen by four
different people during the afternoon. Three of them
noticed him strolling round the church, but not
paying any special attention to the door more than
any other part—or not letting himself be noticed
doing it, at any rate—and one saw him walking on the
hill overlooking the Abbey, about four o'clock. This
one says he was carrying binoculars. One of those
who saw him in the church is quite positive that he
had a small camera, and was photographing the few

bits of medieval carving inside there. He remembers the flash bulbs going off. Incidentally, Bracewell expressly told Cressett that he hadn't brought a camera with him this time. About five he came back to the hotel, had some tea and sandwiches, and sat around and read the evening paper for a while. He was still there at opening time, and had a drink and another snack at the bar, but said he wouldn't be in to dinner, and asked for a sidedoor key, which in any case Mrs. Lloyd always gives her guests, it's less trouble than having to let them in. It was then getting dark, and also misty. So far we haven't found anyone who actually saw him alive after he left the hotel, which was at about a quarter past seven.

"Found in his room afterwards, his pyjamas, a paperback thriller, toilet and shaving kit, and that's all. Found under the body, his briefcase, containing a number of letters of no particular significance that I can see so far, some from girls, some to do with photographs used by various papers; a fairly strong torch, the binoculars mentioned before, and a number of flash bulbs, filters and other equipment. But no camera! So what? It isn't in his hotel room, it isn't in the briefcase, yet he had it. The evidence is sound. So maybe someone who came on him by night in the south porch not only wanted him out of the way, but also wasn't taking any chances on what he might have on record in that camera. In which case whoever it was would probably remove the film and discard the camera. If he was panicky enough he might even make a mistake and leave some prints on it."

"He wouldn't," said Sergeant Moon pessimistically.

"Well, if he was sure he hadn't, and cool enough, he'd simply drop it somewhere in the churchyard. Where better, once the film was out? So that's one job, find that camera."

"That's for me. Go on, what about the post-mortem? How much can the time be narrowed down?"

"Not nearly enough," admitted George. "Just about what I expected. Reece Goodwin says the man was dead certainly before midnight, probably before eleven, but he won't be more exact than that. We know he was alive at a quarter past seven. That's four hours at least. Maybe we'll manage to narrow it down by finding someone who saw him later. We'll try. He was hit twice, Reece says. I'll spare the medical language, but it adds up to the fact that someone picked up the stone and clouted him with it hard enough to lay him out. He was standing when that blow was struck, and probably stooping forward. It might have killed him, in any case, but X was taking no chances. He hit him again, very carefully and thoroughly, as he lay on the ground. And that was that. Fractured skull—an understatement, it was caved in like a soft-boiled egg. Surprisingly little bleeding, considering. He may have lived approximately fifteen to twenty minutes afterwards, but even if he'd been found at once he'd have died.

"And now we've got little Miss Cressett passing on—quite rightly—this curious legend that some poor wretch of a monk dabbled in black magic four hundred odd years ago, and was knocked off by the devil at the foot of that same door, and in just that attitude, when the sanctuary knocker burned his hand and made him loose his hold. Heaven rejected him, and hell got him. Tell me, Jack, did you ever hear that particular legend about Mottisham Abbey?"

"George, my boy, I never did, to tell you the truth. But don't make too much of that, either, we're prodigal about legends here, we spawn 'em and forget 'em. I could have heard it and paid no heed, a dozen times over. Only I don't think so. Bear it in mind, but don't go overboard about it.''

"The old lady said much the same, apparently. She didn't recall it, but didn't totally reject it. I called round at the Abbey on my way out this morning, Jack, just to check with Robert Macsen-Martel. He confirmed that he had obliged with the story when Miss Cressett inquired. He said it was a tradition in the family, but didn't vouch for it in any other way. Very aloof and indifferent. I asked him how it happened that his mother didn't recognise the tale. He said his mother's memory was not what it once had been, and of course she'd known the story, but she took no stock in such superstitions, and so put them out of mind almost wilfully. Which was more or less what the young one—Hugh—said, too. The mother I didn't see.''

"Few people do," said Sergeant Moon. "She's so aristocratic she's become used to existing alone in a rarefied world. It gets narrower and narrower as you get older. She belongs to an older time in more ways than one, you know—she and the son both. They pay on the nail for everything, and they keep their word. The old man's debts—he ran 'em up time and again, and absconded as soon as things got too hot for him— those two paid off every time, to the last penny. Is that such a barren virtue as it sometimes seems?'' The sergeant came down to earth with an acrobat's agility. "What about the widow? Ghosts, doors and church-yards are all very well, but when a wife's murdered, check up on the husband, and when a husband's murdered, check up on the wife. This solitude would make a sweet cover for a dead ordinary killing from dead ordinary motives.''

"Blonde," said George tersely, "thirty-ish, good-looking, a city tough. Had to be. She works, too. According to friends and neighbours, their marriage ran in the offhand way that sometimes results when both partners go on working after the wedding, with no special end in view except more money. They had rows, plenty of them. Lately she seems to have had occasional men, and he occasional women. But they both stayed jealous. It wasn't any secret, when they felt like it they told the whole block. She didn't weep over him, but she wasn't up to providing much information, either. I'll be seeing her again tomorrow.''

He closed his notes with a brisk slap, and yawned exhaustingly. "We've got a choice. Is this a case about a door, and only incidentally about a man? Or is it a case about a man—this chap Bracewell—and only incidentally about a door? You tell me!''

"I wish I could say the door didn't matter," the sergeant owned mournfully, "I wish I could believe somebody simply copped his enemy here by chance, and left us holding a corpse that isn't ours by right. But something tells me the door genuinely matters. Why should he come back, else? George, I don't like it, I don't like it at all.''

"Neither do I," said George grimly. "And you know who's going to like it least of all, unless I doctor my report? The Chief Constable. You know him, he takes fright at the drop of a hat, if he thinks we're in real trouble he'll yell for the Yard tomorrow morning. And it's got to be tomorrow morning or never. They'll curse us to hell if we fetch them in when everything's congealed like cold mutton fat.''

"George," Sergeant Moon leaned over the table and spoke with intense gravity, "don't let him do it. These are our people, and this is our case, and if the southerners get in on it the whole valley will go to ground. It'll be border warfare all over again, I'm telling you. *Get him to leave it to us!*''

"The door, then, not the man?" said George.

"The door! And I'm staking my reputation!''

CHAPTER 4

ROBERTA BRACEWELL, Bobbie to her friends, opened the front door of her first-floor flat at No. 10 Clement Gardens, at the improbable hour of a quarter to eight on the Friday morning, and stared suspiciously at Dave Cressett across the threshold. Her fair hair was still in rollers, half-concealed beneath a chiffon scarf, and she had not yet put on her office face, but from the neck down she was immaculate in a grey worsted dress, sheer stockings and thick-heeled patent shoes.

"Mrs. Bracewell?"

"Oh!" she said blankly, seeing a stranger on the doorstep, and her eyes narrowed into hostility. "I thought it was the post. What a time to come calling, I must say." She inched the door a little nearer closing in his face. "You're not the press again, are you?"

"No, nothing like that. I tried to telephone you last night, but you weren't answering, and they told me you went out to work, so I thought I'd better get it here before office hours. But maybe you aren't going in to work—if not, I'm sorry I disturbed you so early."

"I'm going in," she said grimly. "I have to live. Nobody's going to pay me big money for the story of my life with Gerry, that I know of—a couple of paras and a picture will be all, if they give me that much. And he didn't leave me much but hire-purchase agreements."

"He left you a car," said Dave simply. "I've just

driven it in from my place, where he brought it for repairs. It's down in the street now, if you'll tell me where you want it I'll bring it in for you.'' There were two wooden garages beside the broad drive of the converted Victorian house, but he had no way of knowing which was Bracewell's. "The police have cleared it, everything's in order.''

"The car!'' she said, astonished. "Will you believe me, I never even thought about his car!'' She looked again, and more intently, at Dave. Her face was regular and well-cut, but pale with the dingy city pallor, and her eyes were illusionless. "You're from there?'' she said. "The place where it happened?''

"Yes, that's right. He had a bit of trouble with his steering, and left the car with me that day. I had it ready for him by evening, but he didn't come for it. The police had to go over it, afterwards, but they've finished with it now, it's all yours.''

"Well, well!'' she said with the ghost of a laugh. "Something salvaged! Pity it had to be just a car, but even a car helps. I must owe you some money, then.'' She set the door wide on a narrow white hall. "You'd better come in. I've got time enough, and I daresay you could do with a cup of coffee, starting out as early as all that.''

Dave stayed where he was. "I haven't put in a bill. It wasn't you who commissioned the job. That's all right.''

Her eyes widened a little. She gave him a long, considering look, and then she smiled. "Come in, anyhow, and have the coffee. You're not the press—and God knows I can't be sure whether I want that lot to come in droves or stay away from me altogether—and you're not the police—not that I can complain, they've been all right—what could they do about it? Still, somebody to talk to who isn't either . . . ''

So he went in. What else could he do? She closed the outer door behind them, and clumped along on her chunky heels to the small, primrose-coloured kitchen, all nylon net and blue and white earthenware on a plastic lace tablecloth. The flat was small, hesitant in style, confused in taste, as if she had composed it in hurried five-minute frenzies between the office and whatever her social life consisted of, and forgotten it all the rest of the time. Quite a bit of money had gone into it, but not much effort or thought, and it must surely have been coming to pieces in sheer discouragement long before Gerry Bracewell got himself murdered in some obscure cause in a far-distant village. Yet there were signs that this woman could have been a house-proud wife and mother if she had ever given herself the chance.

She swept her discarded apron from one of the two yellow plastic-upholstered chairs at the kitchen table to make a place for him, and poured him coffee, and then refilled her own cup and sat down opposite him at the table, spreading her arms on the cloth.

Abruptly but quietly she asked: "Did you see him?"

Dave did not even pretend to misunderstand her. "I found him."

"I see!" She lowered her eyes. "Poor old Gerry," she said after a moment, with resigned composure. "He was a bastard to me, but he didn't deserve that. Maybe he wasn't any more of a bastard to me than I was to him, when it comes down to it. How do I know? It just went sour, what does it matter now whose fault it was? I tell you, though, if we had it to do again we wouldn't set about it the same way, I'd see to that. Not that there's ever likely to be a second chance. I don't even want any family now. Leave it, we said, we won't get caught like some of the kids do, not even a year having fun and in come the brats and

the bills, and most likely the debt-collectors, too. Not
for us, thanks! We'll both keep working, we said, get
some capital, get *things*, enjoy life, plenty of time for
settling down when we've had a fling. Trouble is, you
get to like having a fling, and it goes on and on, and
you don't want to let go of it, and all of a sudden . . . ''
She let the hypothetical case slip away from her; her
face tightened, staring stonily at her own situation.
''All of a sudden you're a widow, and he's on a slab
in a mortuary.''

''I'm sorry!'' said Dave helplessly, both cold hands
cupped round his mug of coffee, which if instant was
at least hot. He didn't know what else to say.

She darted him a brief, shrewd glance. ''I know
what you're thinking: *Her* heart's not broken, by a
long chalk. And no more it is. What's the use of
pretending? We haven't mattered much to each other
for a long time. Having a fling got pretty boring
together, he found himself other partners. It's all
right, the police know it all, it doesn't mean a thing
now, but I told them, anyhow. Sure we had rows,
rows all the time. He went off for days when he felt
like it, and there was always a girl behind it. Only last
week we had a row again—how was I to know it was
going to be the last one ever? There was this girl he
used to know, a few years ago . . . she did feature
articles for one of the magazines he used to do pictures
for. They worked together a lot, around five or six
years ago. She'd do interviews with people, or pieces
about places, and he'd do the art work. And last
week, after he was up there in your part of the world,
suddenly he started looking for her again. He thought
I didn't know, but I did. He went to the magazine
offices—I know because he came in with an old
number from way back, and sat down with it and
started thumbing through it as though he expected to
find her telephone number, and then he swore and

threw the thing across the room, because whatever it was he was looking for, he hadn't found it. But when I went to pick it up he made good and sure he got there first. I saw the date, though, it was some time in 1964. They did a whole series together that year, I knew then there was something between them. Then he walked out, and didn't come back until the Friday, and not a word to be got out of him, all he did all the weekend was turn out all his old pictures and slides, hunting for something. I might as well not have been here . . . I might as well have been dead.'' The word shocked her into silence for a moment. She contemplated it bleakly, and accepted it: ''And now he's dead.''

''Did you tell the police all this?'' Dave asked.

''I told them everything I could think of, my whole life story, not that I suppose it means anything now. I told them where I was Tuesday night, too, but how do you prove you were in a cinema? Not even a local, but in the city. From a quarter to five, when I left the office, I could have been anywhere. I didn't come home. What for, I knew he wouldn't he here!'' Her pallid, unmasked morning face had quickened into painful and positive life. Whatever was left of it now, once she had been in love with her husband, and for all her disillusionment she still had not broken the habit of reckoning with him—or, as now, with the blank where he had been.

''But you did tell them about this business with the magazine?'' Dave insisted. ''Because he must have had a reason for hunting up an issue six years old.''

Surprise came as a relief to her. She looked up at him with fresh animation. ''You really think it could mean something? I did tell them, yes, but I didn't make all that much of it. I never thought . . . Here, wait a minute! You could do something for me, at that.''

She got up quickly, and clacked out of the kitchen with more spring to her step than he had yet heard in it; and in a moment she was back with a limp and dog-eared magazine in her hand, *Country Life*-size, once glossy.

"I didn't give them this yesterday because I didn't know where it was. I thought he'd taken it away with him, but he hadn't, he'd only hidden it. I was turning out his papers and letters last night, after they'd gone. I found this shoved at the back of his transparency files. You're going back there anyhow—give it to that inspector for me."

She put it into his hands. He had occasionally seen copies of it before, but half of it was social gossip, provincial at that, and lacking for him both general and local interest, and he had never bought a copy himself in his life. *The Midland Scene*—glossy monthly published right here in Birmingham, but belonging rather to the outer shires than to the city. July 1964, and consequently full of regattas, tennis, gardens open to the public, stately homes on show, and country race meetings. In the winter it would be hunt balls, meets, the exploits of midland skiers abroad, winter sports and annual dinners. The paper was good, the layout elaborate, the colour-printing first-class. He turned the pages, full of social events and comments that seemed to him as remote as Mars; and he came to a feature article with pictures, the centre-piece of the colour pages:

COUNTRY HOUSES OF THE MIDLANDS.
Number Five: MOTTISHAM ABBEY,
MIDSHIRE.

There was no mistaking that long, lofty roof, that thick block of chimneys. The photographs were good and well printed, and had caught house and garden at their summer best. There were two shots of the exterior, one focused across all that remained of a wall of the refectory, barely breaking the soil, one from the best corner of the garden, over a jungle of roses. The lichen-yellows and sage-greens in the roof tiles made an exotic print; and that tall, erect, distinguished-looking fellow in the authentic country tweeds and leather elbows, with wild grey hair still curly and crisp as heather, was Robert Macsen-Martel, senior, a year or so before his death. Sixty years old, but looking at least ten years younger, with a smile that could fetch the birds out of the bushes—literally, according to Saul Trimble.

Dave turned the page, and found a central double-page spread with three more pictures: the dove-cote in the garden, the panelled hall, the drawing-room.

Not the wine-cellar door! Was that the point? Was that what Bracewell had been hoping to find?

He turned back to the previous page. "Text by Alix Trent. Pictures by Gerry Bracewell."

"It's the house up there, where it happened, isn't it?" said Bobbie Bracewell, watching him narrowly.

"Yes, this is the house. The one the door came from."

"That's what I thought. So the police ought to have this. I don't know whether it means anything—but it meant something to *him*, all right. Or something that *isn't* there meant something to him. Take it back with you."

"All right, if that's what you want." He hesitated, aware suddenly of her peculiar desolation, which had not been created, but only revealed, by the loss of a husband. "If it's any consolation, I don't think he was looking for this Alix Trent—or not for her own sake. If he went to the trouble to get this back-number from somewhere, after all this time, it was for these pictures. When he was on a job like that, I suppose he'd take a fair number of pictures, and the author or

the editor would choose the ones they wanted to use?
There'd be more than just these few?''

"Sometimes he'd take as many as thirty to get
three, provided the magazine was paying for everything.''

"And after he'd looked at these, and failed to find
what he wanted, he started turning out all his own
files again?''

She shook her head sadly. ''That wouldn't do him
any good, either. He never kept any but his few best
negatives more than about three years, not where the
work was commissioned. What space would he have
for filing thousands of pictures in a place like this? He
was always going to have a proper filing system and a
proper library some day. When our ship came in—
only we spent too much time pushing the boat out!''
She laughed, and was again grave. ''I'll have to go
and put my face on, it's time I went. But I suppose I
could have a look through them, just in case . . . ''

"Yes, do that,'' said Dave, and got up from the
kitchen table. ''Thanks a lot for the coffee. Now just
tell me where I can put the car for you, and I'll be
getting back.''

He walked away from Number 10 Clement Gardens,
towards the nearest bus-stop, and he had never been
so glad that he wasn't married. The last thing she had
said to him, as he left, was: ''Call in again some time,
if you're this way. You're welcome any time.'' And
the kindling spark he had seen in her eye might have
been merely the stimulus of preparing for the day's
work, but might equally well have been the first signal
of a reviving interest in men—all those men who were
still alive and not on a slab in the mortuary. Whatever its source, it made up his mind for him that he
was never going to call in at Number 10 again. He
didn't dislike her, he was sincerely sorry for her, she

even inspired a sort of respect by her rigorous honesty; but he was never going to see her again if he could help it. He'd take her magazine to Sergeant Moon or to Chief Inspector Felse, and he hoped she'd go through all those negatives and transparencies her husband had kept—at least it would give her an interest for an evening or two, and help her over the worst, even if she found nothing—but from this on, let the police take care of anything she produced.

But the magazine under his arm bothered him. Here was confirmation, if nothing more, that Gerry Bracewell had seen something that puzzled, intrigued and excited him about that church door at St. Eata's, and had wanted desperately to hunt up the pictures he had once made of the house in which the door had then hung. To compare? To confirm some nagging suspicion in his own mind that there was something changed about it? Could he have forgotten, in six years, exactly what pictures he *had* taken? Was it only a shot in the dark that there *might* have been a photograph of that door in its old position? Or did he *know* he'd photographed it? As many as thirty pictures to get three, his wife had said. He couldn't remember which of his batch the magazine had chosen, he had to get hold of a copy of the article first. When that failed, what next? The negatives, presumably, would belong to *The Midland Scene*. So the next step would be— supposing the whole thing was urgent enough, and promising enough—to consult their records. Another disappointment? After he'd thrown the magazine across the room in fury and frustration he'd disappeared until the Friday, and only after that had he settled down grimly to turn out all his dead, past pictures, just in case he'd missed it. So before Friday he'd thought of something and someone else he might try. And drawn another blank.

Who or what filled in that gap? Alix Trent? The

author of the series might well possess prints of all the pictures concerned, but apparently she hadn't storage space, either. And the picture wasn't her work, only an illustration by someone else, she had no copyright in it, why keep it?

All he had to do was get off the bus and make his way to New Street station, and go home. And so he would have done, if the editorial offices of *The Midland Scene* had not been so close to the city centre, and he had not had at least half an hour to wait for a train.

The office was in a new glass and concrete block, smart, sterile and cold, with a fountain and the pillars of Baalbek in the hall; but two floors up, where *The Midland Scene* lived, the premises had settled down into a practical workaday scale and style. A minute front office housed only a receptionist and a telephonist. Dave asked after Alix Trent, and where he could contact her in connection with one of her articles. The receptionist willingly explained that Miss Trent was not on the magazine's pay-roll, but was a freelance who often did work for them, and the office would naturally forward any communications to her. Dave was duly grateful for the information, but had thought of getting in touch with Miss Trent personally while he was here in town—if, of course, she lived in Birmingham. The receptionist examined him sternly through her iris-tinted butterfly glasses, and pondered whether he looked a proper person to be given Miss Trent's address. She was a nice girl, about eighteen and a half by the look of her, with a head of smooth blue-black hair like a well-groomed rook, and the scimitar points of her raven wings stabbed her pink cheeks and made hollows there. She looked over her glasses, because she could see better that way. On the whole, she thought he looked a harmless creature; and Miss Trent was known to be capable of dealing with most eventualities.

"It's in Handsworth, close to the park, I'll write it down for you." Which she did, earnestly.

Dave thanked her, and hesitated. "Look, would you mind telling me—are you on here regularly?"

"Yes, days," she said, and took off her glasses altogether, the better to consider him.

"Do you know if anyone inquired after Miss Trent here last week? I believe a friend of mine may have called in on the same errand."

He must have sounded casual enough and innocent enough. She pondered, visibly turning back the pages of her memory.

"Well, yes, one person did—but I don't think that could be the one you're thinking of, it was one of the photographers who sometimes works for us. He used to work with Miss Trent quite a lot, so I'm told, a few years back. They told me it was O.K. to tell him." She looked momentarily anxious, but not because death had leaned over her shoulder. She was young, she had something better to do in her spare time than read the crime news.

"No, that wouldn't be my man. Never mind, thanks, anyhow."

"He didn't come just for that, actually," the girl said, "he came to go through our library pictures for something he wanted, but I don't think he found it. We don't keep material that hasn't been used for publication, you see, not for more than a year or so— not unless it's of exceptional interest."

"No, of course not. I suppose space is always a problem."

"These new places," she told him with conviction, "look *huge*, but you try working in them! There isn't room to swing a cat, let alone a camera."

Dave went out and took a bus towards Handsworth from the nearest bus-stop.

At something after ten o'clock, Alix Trent opened

the door of her Edwardian semi wide, as only large-minded people do, and looked at her unexpected visitor with mild inquiry. As she stood on her three-inch doorstep, her eyes were exactly on a level with his.

She was the brownest girl Dave had ever seen. Her hair was a weighty long bob, the colour of good tan shoe-polish, and glossy as conkers, her lashes and brows were the same tint with an added relish of red, her forehead and cheeks were matt brown in an indescribable shade, flushed with rose and fading into ivory. She wore a shirt-dress in a tint very like her own complexion, saddle-stitched with dark brown, and in the collar she had a gossamer scarf in bright apricot. Her shoes were tan, coffee and cream in a series of fragile straps. Her features were wry and friendly, not at all beautiful, apart from the deep-brown, luminous eyes, which so far remained distantly grave though her large, generous mouth smiled at him.

"Miss Trent?" Dave inquired, and his tone was almost incredulous, so far removed did this girl seem from the racy rival Bobbie Bracewell had been imagining, and so extremely unlikely ever to have had any but business connections with Gerry Bracewell.

"Yes, I'm Alix Trent."

Her voice was low-pitched, brisk and pleasant, with a note of good-humoured patience in it. He had interrupted her at work, but he didn't look the type to do so without reason.

"If you could spare me just a few minutes I should be very much obliged. My name's Cressett. I'm not the police or the press or anything official, and I haven't any standing, but it's about Gerry Bracewell's death." He saw by her face that she did read the papers, and that she would never be able to feel completely disinterested about the murder of someone she had known and worked with. "I got involved," he said, "whether I wanted to or not. I found him. And I've just come from his widow."

That struck two notes at once with her; her face was mobile and expressive, she was sorry for Bobbie Bracewell, but also she knew how she herself had been regarded in that quarter, and his coming from the widow could mean several very different things.

"There's a matter of a feature article you and he handled together," Dave said carefully, "which seems to be connected in some way with his death. Or at least the house in it does. I believe he came to see you before he was killed."

"Yes," she said readily and coolly, "he did come to see me."

"Don't misunderstand me—you, his visit to you—this has nothing to do with the case. Only the matter about which he wanted to see you, this *is* relevant. At least, *I* think so."

"But you are not the police," she said reasonably, and for the first time almost smiled at him with her eyes as well as her lips.

"This is something the police don't yet know, but will as soon as I get back today. His widow gave me this to take back to them." He held out the magazine for her to see, and her understanding was candid, neutral and detached. "I thought I might, with luck, be able to take more at the same time. Will you help me?"

"Forgive me," she said, aware that her smile was getting a little out of hand, "but you do appear such an improbable amateur detective."

"I'm not one," he said shortly, "I don't want to be one, I never shall be one. I'm just the man who found the body, and I happen to belong—I mean *belong*—to the small, closed community where it happened. I don't like a man being wiped out anywhere, and especially not in our village. And I don't like unpaid debts hanging round the necks of innocent people. I want right done, that's all.''

A long time afterwards, when they knew each other very much better, she told him that what had impressed her most of all, and made up her mind for her there and then about more matters than one, was that the word he used was not ''justice'', but ''right''. A distinction so narrow and so profound.

''Come in!'' said Alix, and set the door wide.

She listened to everything he had to say, and he said much more than he had realised was necessary, because she was a good listener, intent, responsive, with the patience to wait for a slower but possibly more powerful and accurate mind than her own to find the words it needed without prompting. She kept very still while he talked, and she thought deeply and talked openly when it was her turn. Once she had made up her mind there were no half-measures.

''Yes, you're right, of course, he did come to me. After he'd found nothing in the archives, I suppose. He wanted to know if I'd kept any of the unused pictures from that country house series. He didn't say which one he was interested in at first, and if I'd had anything to show him I don't think he'd have committed himself any further. But I don't keep past material, except file copies of my own work. And it hadn't seemed likely that there'd be any future sales in that particular set, they were commissioned, and nobody else was going to show interest. As I remember it, all the houses were much the same—after all, the major ones are too well known, it was the small stuff we were concerned with. These tumbledown dumps miles from anywhere, with arthritis in every flagstone—So when it was clear I had nothing to show, then he did begin to probe in another way. That was the first time he actually mentioned Mottisham Abbey. I read the papers, I knew about the door being put back into the church porch, it didn't take much guessing to decide that he'd been covering the ceremony. He started reminding me of what the house was like, and asking how much I remembered. In the end it came down to what he really wanted. How well did I remember the wine-cellar door.''

She looked up at Dave, across her plain, practical, uncluttered workroom, and smiled. Smiling made her mouth slightly oblique, one corner flicking engagingly upwards.

It sounded hopeless. One house in a series of at least five, one minor feature in the house, one visit . . . ''It was expecting a lot,'' Dave owned ruefully.

''As it happens, I had some reason to remember it, though not enough to be much use to him, apparently. I do remember it was a nice piece of carving, though very dark and coated with a rather nasty varnish . . .''

''They've removed that,'' said Dave.

''Good for them! It did look well worth cleaning up. But nobody said a word about any legends attaching to it, not to us, at any rate. Of course, it was the old man himself who showed us round, and he wasn't the kind to retail legends, from what we saw of him. He scoffed at the whole thing. I was slightly offended, to tell the truth, after all I was twenty-three then, and took my job very seriously, and I expected patrician elderly gentlemen to take their historic houses seriously, too. He didn't. He told me exactly what he thought of old, cold, insanitary stone houses, and said if my rag thought so highly of the place they could have it, he was only waiting for a reasonable offer. He was a character. And handsome, too. Not to say oncoming! What I chiefly remember about the wine-cellar is that he contrived to close the door—or partially close it—with himself and me inside, while Gerry was making some shots of the outside.''

''Then he *did* photograph the door?'' Dave interrupted quickly.

''Oh, yes, both he and I were quite sure of that, that's why he was hunting for the prints, but none of us had kept them—they weren't used, as you've seen. And when we were alone inside there, not to make a long story of it, old Mr. Martel made a very debonair but very determined pass at me, and I had to whip the door open pretty smartly and make a discreet getaway. The things I know about that door are not so much visual, consequently. What I remember most is how surprised I was, considering its size, at the sweet way it swung. Whoever hung it knew his business. It balanced beautifully, even though it wasn't all that well cared for, and creaked a little in motion.''

It sounded absolutely authentic. Given the late Robert's reputation, it would have been unthinkable for him to be shut in a cellar with an attractive twenty-three-year-old girl and not make a pass at her. He would have considered it an opportunity wasted, almost a dereliction of duty.

''But nothing else strikes you about the door as you remember it?—the door or the knocker?''

She shook her head. ''I'm sorry! If only I knew what sort of something, even!''

''If only I could tell you,'' he agreed ruefully. ''Well, thanks, anyhow. I shall have to pass on all this to the police. You won't mind?''

The heavy, smooth cap of russet hair swung again. ''I don't mind. I'll keep thinking about it. Something might occur to me.''

He knew he had interrupted her in the middle of a job, there was paper in the typewriter on the desk at the window, and a sheaf of loose pages beside it to be copied. He knew he ought to go, and was even aware that he would be well advised to go now, if he intended ever to come this way again. The time for knowing her better was not yet; but it would come.

"Yes, do keep it in mind. If you think of anything that even may be significant, would you let the Midshire C.I.D. know about it?" He had the wit not to ask her to regard him as the natural intermediary, and send her afterthoughts to him.

She had risen with him, to accompany him to the door. She had a long, free, self-reliant step, and when she gave him her hand it was significant, the seal on an agreement. At the last moment, before he turned towards the gate and she closed the door, she said with deliberation: "A photograph might help, if your local paper carried one. Look in, when you're in town again, and if you've got a picture, bring it with you."

It was the measure of her impact that there was no echo at all. Bobbie Bracewell might never have existed. All he felt was that simple and exhilarating lift of the heart assuring him that he would see Alix Trent again, that it was she who was making the approach easy for him.

"I will," he said, and walked away from her down the path with *The Midland Scene* under his arm, and a sense of sudden achievement flooding his senses, as though the sun had come out.

CHAPTER 5

GEORGE FELSE stood under the arching trees that shadowed the south porch of St. Eata's, in the first fine drizzle of rain, and stared at the wreath of wilted, greyish-green herbage that sagged on the sanctuary knocker. The head of the mythical beast, inanely grinning, jutted out of the tired greenery like a clown from a wilted muslin ruff, obscenely mocking the gravity of the beholders. Withdrawn, the village moved about stealthily in circles, eyes slanted always towards the profaned place of death, feet always directed assiduously somewhere else. There wasn't a soul for two miles round who didn't know.

The dark-green, crinkled leaves drooped despondently, as if they held out very little hope that they would be effective in warding off the obscure evil from outside human experience—which was hypothetically the purpose for which someone had placed them there. It was even something of an achievement to get hold of that much parsley in October, let alone hang it in position in this most exposed of places without being caught in the act. Though a soul benevolent enough to be scheming for the protection of this troubled place against all evil spirits should also have been indifferent to observation. Unless, of course, by demons, whose attentions it would be reasonable enough to avoid if possible.

"All right," said George philosophically, "you didn't see anyone, you don't know anything. I get it. But you do know what this is for, don't you? Avaunt, ye spirits of chaos, spawn of darkness, malicious powers, make yourselves scarce! This is no place for you, this is a place protected. All right, you can unhook it now, it's served its purpose.''

"I dursen't, sir,'' said Ebenezer Jennings without a blush, and stood by George's side in full daylight to be surveyed, his face as hard as the building stone they had once quarried from the western slope of Callow, now long overgrown in bracken and furze. ''That's magic, sir. That's good magic. I don't meddle with yon. This church is troubled bad, and that garland, that's blessed. Yes, I do know what virtue's in these leaves. You leave 'un there, I say. That ain't no ill, is it? Leave 'un be, and hope!''

George wondered, in one instant of mental irresponsibility, whether it was the mere fact of the man's office as verger, or something in his remarkable appearance, that enabled him to get away with that kind of language without being ridiculous. He was almost sure that it was not because of any actual belief he had in these things; on the contrary, the whole delivery had something of the impressiveness of a first-class theatrical performance, larger than life and double as natural. The office of verger was practically hereditary in Mottisham; and this was the role that went with it, the trappings, the privilege.

Eb Jennings the Fifth was a man of medium height and inordinate dryness, all stout bones and leathery hide without much flesh between. He looked as if the wind might blow him away, but he was as tough as old boots. His head was large, with a lofty, domed skull bristling with long grey hair, his face all forehead, tapering away down a long nose to a narrow, hanging jaw, and his eyes in their gaunt sockets burned with a dark, prophetic fire. He would not have been out of place in the direst books of the Old Testament. Even in ancient flannels blotched with paint and grease, and a washed-out oiled-wool sweater, beginning to unravel at the hem, he was impressive.

"And how can you be sure it was put there to protect?" George asked curiously, watching the verger's lantern of a face. "Oh, yes, we know that's what it means, or what it's supposed to mean, but what if whoever put it there did it to frighten the whole village half to death, on the principle of 'the mair mischief the mair sport'? That wouldn't be much benefit to anybody except the murderer, would it? If he stirred up enough muck he might escape notice in the obscurity. Might even be left free to make his next move, whatever that may be. You live here at the lodge on the corner of the churchyard, don't you? Right in the danger zone!"

A boy of about eighteen or nineteen came butting through the gathering rain, shears in hand, and dived into the porch beside them just in time to hear this. George had seen him clipping back the encroaching ivy from the north wall before the shower began.

"Don't you waste your time trying to scare this old raven," he said, punching Jennings lightly in the ribs, and dropping the shears on to the bench inside the porch. "I'd be sorry for the demon that tried tangling with him, I tell you."

"You mind your own business," Eb Jennings told him smartly, "and don't interrupt your elders and betters."

"And don't let him kid you he takes any stock in this Dracula stuff," went on the boy, undeterred, nodding a shaggy, light-brown head at the dangling wreath. "He's got his own recipes." He sat down beside his shears, and leaned to examine the withering leaves more closely. His lively lips curled in tolerant disdain. "You know there's a couple of London cranks from some psychic research gang booked in at the 'Arms' last night? And a folklore collector from Birmingham? As well as a few national press folks. Somebody slipped the word out there were devils loose up here.''

"Somebody," said George, "certainly did." He was less concerned about that particular somebody. The murderer was hardly likely to want professional observers on the scene, however effectively they might embarrass the police; they were all too likely to turn up something he wanted to remain buried. But the man who hung up a clear alarm signal on the spot could well be the murderer himself, studying to redouble confusion, while he himself withdrew farther into the undergrowth. "Good for the hotel trade, at any rate.''

"Maybe Mrs. Lloyd hung up the parsley," suggested the boy cheerfully. "Bait for the ghost-hunters!''

"Only fools mock at the presence of evil," said Eb Jennings reprovingly, scowling at the boy, whose long legs spread across the porch almost to the bench on the other side.

"Why not, if propitiation does no good? You might as well die laughing." He patted the purring iron beast. "Caution, guard dogs on patrol!''

"I will not stay," said Jennings magnificently, "to listen to impious talk. You'll excuse me, Mr. Felse, I've got work to do." And as he made his exit through the church, that being the driest way, he looked back at the boy and said, making a lightning return to everyday practicality: "And since you've been druv in by the rain, you can go and get some wood in for your mother.''

He was gone, leaving the knocker swaying gently, and rustling as the leaves brushed the door. He also left his own minor shock still almost palpable on the air. George told himself that he ought to have guessed. There was something in their wrangling, teasing, needling exchanges that yet stopped short of all malice, and argued a very considerable area of understanding between them. And yet they were, physically, so strikingly unlike.

The boy was more than a head the taller, elegantly long and loose-knit and athletic, with straight fair hair and blue-grey eyes. His face, too, was elongated, but in suave curves, and with a lot of shapely bone; a high-bridged nose jutted haughtily, and brows level as the pommel of a sword underlined a broad forehead. He was looking straight back at George, well aware of what he must be thinking, and visibly speculating as to whether he would or would not ask. Which made it imperative to ask bluntly or not at all.

"So he's your father?"

"Well," said the boy with cheerful deliberation, "by courtesy he is. And anyhow, I'd sooner be Jennings, than Macsen-Martel."

"Like that, is it?" If the boy was willing to accept the conversation on this level, so was George. "You're the wild oat I've been hearing about."

"I'm one of them," said the boy drily. "When you've been around here a bit longer you'll learn to spot this debased Norman pan."

"He's left more of you around?"

"Brother," said the boy reverently, "he could field a football team." The blue-grey eyes flashed in an impudent but engaging smile. "And probably a netball team as well. You ask Sergeant Moon." He got up, hoisting the shears from where he had laid them. "I suppose I'd really better go and get some wood in for my mother—it's set in for the day, by the look of it." And he walked away unconcernedly through the rain, weaving his way blithely among the graves to take the nearest line to the lodge, and whistling as he went, and George saw in this rear view of him the tall, wide-shouldered, narrow-flanked shape and long gait of the Macsen-Martels, unmistakable in movement where he might have missed it completely in repose. One of the family strays, but one that had found a good home. There was nothing the matter with the relationship between courtesy father and son; and what was further implied was that the situation had been accepted by both of them from the beginning. Ask Sergeant Moon! Not bad advice in the circumstances.

There was moss wound into the parsley wreath, and there was the grit of soil and the remains of an ochreous moisture in the moss. Better let the laboratory have a go at it, they might be able to suggest the locality from which it had come, and if the spirit-hunters had begun to arrive, that might not be Mottisham at all. Either some superstitious crank or earnest student of the occult had really put it there in an effort to guard the church and the community against evil spirits, or the murderer had attempted a piece of conjurer's misdirection to divert attention from his own solid humanity and his entirely earthly motives. No, on reflection there was, regrettably, the third possibility: someone who enjoyed trouble and chaos had simply added his own contribution to the brew here out of pure devilment. Of that kind of devil even villages as remote as Mottisham have more than enough.

George turned up the collar of his coat and made a dash for it through what had now become a downpour, across the road and into the vicarage drive. In the gateway he collided with a young man who had just descended from the Comerbourne bus and made for the same haven. They steadied each other solicitously with hasty apologies, and recognition was instant and mutual.

"I was just coming to see you, Mr. Felse," said

Dave Cressett, hugging *The Midland Scene* under his jacket from the driving rain, "I've got something here Mrs. Bracewell asked me to bring to you. And something besides to tell you."

"Always the door," said Sergeant Moon, late that Friday evening, after they had abandoned the mounds of official reports and statements, and were sitting back relaxed and tired over cigarettes and beer, thoughtfully brought in from the "Duck" by young Brian Jennings. "I'd be ready to bet my job that we were right, it's the door, not the man. He just blundered into something he didn't realise was dangerous—apparently merely by having this feeling that there was something odd about this door he'd once photographed for this magazine article. Now you tell me what dangerous secret there can be about an oak door? Worth killing for?"

"And before he'd even run to earth whatever it was he was after," George pointed out. "A very dangerous secret indeed—show a little too much interest in it, and that's enough, you're knocked off just in case. Yet there was plenty of interest being shown in it—by all kinds of people. It was ceremonially on show. So what was so different about this man Bracewell's interest, to mark him out as the chance that couldn't be taken?"

"He was there prowling around it at night," said Moon, "and alone. A crowd with a battery of cameras was O.K. One man with a torch sneaking back by himself wasn't."

"There was one more thing about him that was different, Jack. *He'd seen it before.*"

Moon considered that carefully. For centuries the door had hung in the cellars of the Abbey. The house had never been shown; and it was improbable that there had ever been more than one such article about it as the one in *The Midland Scene*. It wasn't important enough or beautiful enough; it played too insignificant a part in history. The wonder was that it had achieved a place even once in such a series. That made Bracewell, in all probability, the only person present at the re-dedication, apart, of course, from the family, who had ever seen the door in its previous position.

"But even so, what could there have been about it to make him think he might get a scoop out of it? Something he hadn't noticed until the thing was cleaned up? But then it would be there for everyone to notice. Whatever was queer about it meant nothing to anyone but him."

"And what discoveries can you make about a door, for God's sake? There it is, a solid block of wood with a lump of iron attached, everything about it visible at a glance." George stretched and yawned. "Well, I'll see this Miss Trent tomorrow, and have another word with Mrs. Bracewell. Who knows, I may hit on the right question by sheer luck, and stir a recollection, or she may have thought of something on her own. We've no choice about pulling out all the stops now, Jack. It took some hard work to get the Old Man to leave it with us, we've got to justify it now or die trying."

"Well, at least we found the camera. Not that I expect the lab boys will get anything off it." And of course it had been empty, the film extracted, and no doubt burned long before this. "There's just a chance he'd *have* to take off his gloves to open and close the camera properly, but I'm not betting on it. It's a smooth one to handle. And me with five chaps combing the place for it," said Sergeant Moon sadly, "and it had to be young Brian who found it!"

The camera had been half-buried in the debris of dead flowers where old wreaths were dumped, in the most deserted corner of the graveyard. If Brian had not been tidying up the dump that morning, and happened to kick against metal, it might have taken them at least another day to work their way to it.

"It's true, is it," George asked, "that Robert Macsen-Martel—the late Robert, that is—left a trail of bastards all round these parts? Brian," he explained wryly, "chose to account for himself. Quite frankly. According to him there are plenty more."

"True enough. But the Jennings family, now, they're a special case. Those three get on so well together, you wouldn't believe. That's what I call coming to terms with reality. You haven't seen the mother, have you? She's only thirty-nine now, and still as pretty as new paint. Linda Price, she was, went as maid to the Abbey—her old man must have been daft to let her. Nineteen, and a stunner, she was then. Exactly what you'd expect happened. Old Jennings, he's twenty years older than her, he was a widower, and he had a soft spot for Linda. A sort of honourable bargain it was, and they've both kept it. He married her, and took on her boy—and gladly, I may say, his first wife never had any, and Linda's never had any since, so it looks as if but for her slip-up he hadn't a chance of getting a son. She's never looked at anyone but old Eb since, she thinks the sun shines out of his high forehead. They got off lucky, all of 'em, they know how to value one another, even if they are a rum bunch. There's many a family round here started off with a romantic love affair, and ended up with squabbling parents and problem children, and here's the Jennings lot starting off with a business arrangement and ending as snug as old lovers, with an only child who hasn't got so much as a complex or an inhibition to his name. Others," said the sergeant sombrely, "weren't so clever. There's fathers round this valley that know their kids aren't theirs, and make them pay for it, and what's more, get it back off the kids with interest. And there's others that don't even know, and might very well do murder if they ever found out."

"Not, however, this murder," sighed George. "Plenty of reason for nursing grudges against the Martel clan, but what had this poor devil done?" He pondered for a moment, and human curiosity got the better of him. "Any special cases in mind? Locally?"

Sergeant Moon turned towards the window. Faintly through the wet trees beamed the distant lights of "The Duck", and a mere murmur of music drifted in from the jukebox in the garden bar.

"Some time," he said, "when you're at leisure, go and take a good close look at Nobbie Crouch."

"They're taking the copper off guard tonight," Saul Trimble said, flicking a beer-mat accurately in front of Joe Lyon and dumping a levelled-off pint of home-brewed on it without spilling a drop. He deposited his own pot carefully, for the corner table tended to rock slightly, but he knew his territory so well that it was no hazard to him. "Got to give the lads a few hours off in the end, and nothing's happened so far, has it? I reckon even the spooks are bound to have a bit o' respect for the English week-end. Back on duty a' Monday."

He had an uncanny instinct for choosing the role that would most surely provoke whatever strangers he had hooked for the bar's entertainment. Everyone had taken it for granted that the earnest researchers who had taken rooms at the hotel would carry their inquiries, after opening time, into the bar of "The Sitting Duck". The natives did not use "The Martel Arms". The reason was beer rather than caste, but the aliens were not to know that. They came slumming, and it was a wonder they didn't bring their tape recorders with them, so quaint and primitive was

Sam Crouch's antiquated—and profitable—bar, and so renowned its characters. The visitors being believers, Saul had become a sceptic of the bleakest kind. He believed in nothing he could not touch, smell or drink. He deposited his lean rump in the red pulpit-cushions of the corner settle, and winked at Dinah Cressett across the crowded bar.

This was Saturday night, so everyone was there. The general hum of conversation—"The Sitting Duck" was never a noisy bar, they banished the young and loud into the garden pavilion—was constant, drowsy and warm, like the busy signature of a hive of bees. Over this background, dominant voices floated in emphatic moments like soloists in opera soaring out of the chorus, to subside again gracefully without breaking the continuous arc of rounded, communal sound. Not many pubs can command such orchestration and balance, these days.

"The mockers," pronounced Eb Jennings, in an unexpected bass lead-in that seemed to emerge from the cellars under their feet, "the mockers may have blood on their hands by morning. Who took away the wreath that was meant to protect us all?"

On Saturday nights the Jennings family went their separate ways, each member with the family blessing on his choice: Eb to the bar of the "Duck", Linda to the Bingo in the infant school, with her friend Mrs. Bowen, and young Brian, on his powerful pest of a motor-bike, to the weekly dance in Comerbourne, replete with beat groups blessed with incredible names, and heady with nubile girls. Brian was a heroic dancer and a Spartan motor-cyclist. His gear was stark, immaculately maintained and without insignia. In transit he looked more like one of Cocteau's symbolic fates pursuing Orpheus than a modern, brass-knobbed, long haired, seedy enthusiast.

Within the memories of the regulars, however, Eb

had never taken any active part in the entertainments staged impromptu at the "Duck". Either something had got into him, tonight, or else this was the first occasion that had touched him nearly, and caused him to give tongue.

"In the midst of life," he proclaimed, erect beside the bar like a prophetic angel, even his pint forgotten, "in the midst of life we are in death. Like our brother departed. No one should laugh who is not ready to go."

For one instant he achieved such an impression that there was total silence in the bar. Then Saul said reasonably: "Well, nobody who's ready to go is going to feel much like laughing, that's for sure. And anyhow, you tell the police, Eb, lad, don't tell us, *we* didn't shift your parsley garland."

"Nor call the coppers off night watch," confirmed Willie the Twig. "After all, they've kept a guard on the church for three nights, and nothing happened. And they need plenty of men during the day on these jobs, they can't wear out a constable minding the scene of the crime indefinitely."

"Anyhow," said Eli Platt sententiously, "lightning never strikes twice in the same place."

"Have it your way, then," intoned Eb, "but I tell you we're not finished yet with this evil. 'Tis in the air all about us. 'Tis lurking there on the scene where the murder was done. I feel my thumbs prick and my blood chill when I go near that door."

"There's nothing to be afraid of," one of the visitors explained with kindly condescension, "if you approach these phenomena in a scientific spirit. From what you've told us of the past history of the Abbey, this is a very interesting case which ought to be investigated by someone trained in the proper research techniques. What's needed is accurate and detached observation. That's impossible if one is afraid."

Everyone looked at him with the awed respect of the simple villager for the visiting expert. He was a large, slightly flabby man with an egg-shaped skull fringed with reddish hair, and his pale, probing nose was peppered with russet freckles. He was earnest and patronising, and none too free with paying for drinks; but so innocently impervious to all double meanings that Dinah felt it was a shame to take advantage of him.

"I intend," he announced, having drawn all eyes upon himself, "to keep watch myself tonight. Alone!"

He declared himself with all possible ceremony. The effect was pleasing, up to a point. Everyone gaped at him with curiosity, speculation, and—he was sure—admiration. He had hoped also for a degree of anxious solicitude, but of this he could be less certain.

"Sooner you than me, friend," said Willie the Twig, with obliging (and quite mendacious) fervour. He lived alone in the back of beyond with his forests, his Land-Rover and a couple of setters, and habitually patrolled by night unarmed, even when he had reason to believe there were wood—or deer-poachers about; and so far no one had been able to identify anything in any real or imaginary world of which he could be said to be afraid.

"You're venturing too far, 'tis daring the devil," protested Eb, outraged. "You think you're wise, my friend, but 'tis foolishness to walk too proud in the face of powers more than mortal."

"Call it off till it stops raining," offered Saul sportingly, "and we'll make up a party. How about you, Hugh, lad?"

"Not me!" said Hugh, not without regret. "Sorry, but I'm driving in the Mid-Wales rally tomorrow. Got to get my sleep tonight, I shall be off about five in the morning. Any other time you plan a ghost-hunt, I'll be delighted.''

''Oh, ah, that's right, I forgot! Can't afford to risk your chances in the hill run, that's a fact. Anybody else game?''

Facetious offers of help and prophecies of doom came cascading from all directions in bewildering variety. The man from the research society was horrified. These attitudes were the outcome of ignorance, and did untold harm. How could extra-human forces be expected to manifest themselves and communicate where there was derision and noise and lack of understanding? Where no one believed except those who were afraid with the old panic terror, and no one at all had an open mind? He must and would be alone on his watch; it was an opportunity not to be missed. He had brought with him merely a raincoat, a notebook and a torch. His purpose was not to tape-record for his own glory, not to stand off an enemy, but to observe, to report truthfully, and to attempt to establish communication if the opportunity was offered.

''Pity, really, about the Mid-Wales being tomorrow,'' Hugh whispered in Dinah's ear, ''we could have fixed him up with a set of phenomena he'd never forget.''

''Hush!'' Dinah whispered back, smiling and frowning. ''He really means it, you know. In a way there *is* something brave about it.''

''Brave nothing, love! Insensitive and big-headed! It would be gorgeous,'' said Hugh, entranced with the prospect, ''if he really did see something. I bet you wouldn't see him for dust! Our Porsche wouldn't keep his tail-lights in sight!''

That was what was really occupying his mind, Dinah realised, tomorrow, and the twenty-four-hour rally he had a sporting chance of winning. Ted

Pelsall, who was Jenny's brother and their best mechanic, had withdrawn the car a week ago to his own yard, in the ramshackle ex-farmhouse close to the Abbey, and had been working on it lovingly ever since. He always acted as Hugh's navigator, and since they had to make such an early start to reach the muster-point on time, Hugh was sleeping at the Abbey tonight, where Ted would pick him up before dawn. At least his mother would be happy to have him in the house, even if she saw him for only half an hour before retiring to bed. Sometimes, since that strained evening in her company, Dinah thought of his mother with a curious compassion, detached and mature, surprising even to herself.

"We ought to be going soon," she whispered.

"Yes, love, I know . . . " But he went on staring in thoughtful abstraction at the psychic researcher, who was standing his ground with an obstinacy so publicly declared that now it could hardly be retracted. Yet to do him justice, he must have meant it from the beginning, since he had come provided with a packet of sandwiches and a small flask of coffee as well as his raincoat and torch. Retreat before his own accusing eyes would have been even harder than retreat in the face of all the mockery and terrorisation "The Sitting Duck" was exercising upon him. And perhaps he was as stupidly big-headed as Hugh had said. Whatever his motives, scientifically pure or humanly stubborn, he meant to go through with it. He *would* go through with it.

"Drink up, then, my fond and fair one! Sure you wouldn't like the other half?"

"No, really, thanks. We promised Dave we'd cut it short."

Hugh held her coat for her, and they withdrew among a chorus of good nights. Everyone who remembered about the rally added fervent good wishes. One or two even had bets on him. They passed close by the earnest stranger, who was also climbing into his coat with slightly defiant resolution. The torch he fished out of a deep pocket was truly formidable in size. Hugh eyed it respectfully in passing.

"You need that to see the ghosts, or what?"

"They don't like light," said Eb Jennings mysteriously, as if, had he wished, he could have given this amateur a lot of valuable tips.

"He's right, you know," said Hugh seriously. "Much better leave it behind. You're taking this whole thing too lightly. In for a giggle, in for a thrill, if the monks don't get you, the devils will!"

"You're awful!" said Dinah, as they darted through the rain to the car, the everyday Mini they used for general transport. "You just don't give a damn for anybody!"

"Those people burn me up. Coming to a place they know nothing about, and feel nothing about, where if they had sense they'd sit and listen, and put out feelers until they understood at least the language! I can't stand phoneys!"

"I'll drive," said Dinah, slithering behind the wheel, for she had, in any case, to drive herself home from the Abbey after dropping him. They threaded the roads between autumnal, leaning trees, streaming and gleaming with rain. She drove well; both Dave and Hugh had had a hand in teaching her, and her vision was phenomenally sharp and her reactions naturally rapid and decisive. "Take me as navigator," she said suddenly, "I mean next time. Ted wouldn't mind, just for once."

"Ted wouldn't mind anything you suggested, and you know it. Ted dotes. Sometimes I'm downright jealous. You sure you want to run yourself into the ground on a stint like that?"

"I could do it," she said confidently. "I bet I can stick out anything you can."

"If only it hadn't got so damned professional these days, we'd do the Monte together. I'd love it! Dinah, Dinah . . ."

"Hey, cut it out!" protested Dinah, unexpectedly kissed behind the left ear and—by mistake on a curve—in the left eye. "You'll have us in the hedge!"

They turned into the Abbey drive. There were lights in the drawing-room.

"Good, Mother's still up." It was not much after nine o'clock. "She's got a bit of a cold, Rob said, but it probably won't be much. Anyhow, I'll go and give her your love, shall I?"

"Yes," said Dinah, "do that." It wasn't love she felt, but it was something outgoing and grievous and urgent, and the word love would do for want of one more exact. She was sorry for everyone who was old and lonely, and narrow, and cold.

Hugh kissed her, now with a more assured aim, and at leisure. "See you some time Tuesday morning, then."

"Give me a ring when the results are out, I'll be waiting to hear how you got on."

He promised, and disentangled himself reluctantly.

"And go to bed as soon as she does," ordered Dinah, as he got out of the car, "or you'll be dropping tomorrow."

He mouthed one more promise and blew a kiss back to her, and was gone. Dinah turned the car in the broad stretch of unkempt gravel before the door, and drove back home. The rain continued, steady, soft-voiced and impersonal, a curtain of pearl-textured sound against the stillness of the night.

The Saturday night dances in Comerbourne ended, in deference to the English sabbath, at midnight, but in practice no one actually left before half past twelve, even if the extra half hour was spent in gossiping and finishing up the last drinks after the band had gone. Consequently it was regularly after half past one in the morning when Brian Jennings roared back into Mottisham, accompanied by the hearty curses of all the residents he disturbed in passage. Brian considered he was entitled to one anti-social moment in his week, and this was it. He admitted he could have made his machine quieter if he'd cared to, but he just loved the music it made. At about twenty to two on this particular Sunday morning Dave, whose bedroom overlooked the road, heard him thunder by on his way home. About ten minutes later the offence was aggravated by a second disturbance, just as Dave was drifting into sleep again. A handful of gravel rattled sibilantly down the window. Dave rolled out of bed and flung up the sash.

"What the hell do you think . . ."

"Don't shoot, Dave! It's me, Brian Jennings . . ."

There was the slender black figure, anonymous as a skin diver in the P.V.C. overalls he wore over his good suit. As if he felt the need to identify himself beyond question, the boy hurriedly hauled off helmet and goggles, and tilted upwards a tense, wide-eyed face.

"Let me in, will you, please, I've got to use the 'phone. Honest, it's urgent. I didn't want to knock up the Rev., and there's no copper there tonight . . ." His voice was a strenuous whisper, and conveyed just enough of shock and excitement to restrain Dave from argument. Reactions were quick in Mottisham these days.

"What's happened now?"

He kept his voice down, too. Dinah slept on the other side of the house, no need for her to be disturbed.

"There's another one copped it," said Brian tersely. "Only this one isn't dead—not yet . . . "

"I'll come down," said Dave, and vanished from the window.

Brian was pressed against the jamb of the door by the time Dave reached it, and slid inside as soon as it was opened. He was quivering gently, but more with a terrier's excitement in the hunt than with super-stitious alarm. "Sorry about this, I'd have gone straight to the police, but this is the one night there's nobody there . . . I'd better get the doctor first . . . "

"Who is it?" asked Dave, steering him towards the office.

"One of those new chaps—the spook-hunters . . . "

"In the porch, like the other one?" Dave hoisted the telephone from its rest. "Here you are, go ahead, it's your story."

"Right up against the door on his face, just like the first . . . " Brian's hard young finger dialled rapidly and without error. Somewhere distant at the other end of the line a furious but controlled voice addressed him. Doctors are used to being called out at night, and used, moreover, to making the rapid decision as to whether to come or not on the evidence given. On public business Brian talked with the efficiency and authority of one sure of his ground.

"We've got a bad case of injury here at the church at Mottisham, I think it could be a fractured skull—head injuries, anyhow, and he's unconscious. Should I call the ambulance or leave it to you? No, it wasn't an accident, it looks like the last time. I *know*, I *am* getting on to Sergeant Moon as soon as this line's clear . . . If you think I'm fooling, I'll give you Mr. Cressett to talk to if you like.—Right, thanks, I'll be standing by till you come." He held down the rest and began to dial again, flashing a fiery glance at Dave. "They don't trust anybody, do they? '*Is this a hoax, young fellow*?' " He mimicked savagely. "If you're under twenty they think you're missing on one cylinder."

He misdialled in his haste, and swore, and started over again. The sergeant's voice, only slightly furred with sleep, came over the line.

"Brian Jennings here, sergeant, speaking from Cressett's garage." Brian had tensed from head to toes in concentration. "There's another casualty here at the church, same place, same style—I found him about six minutes ago. He isn't dead—at least, he wasn't—I've called the doctor, he's on his way. It's one of those chaps from London, the psychic research blokes . . . And, sergeant—*I saw the chap who hit him*—only a glimpse, it was raining, and black as a bag there, but I saw someone dive out of the porch and make off in the trees. Look, you're not going to like this," said Brian apologetically, "and I don't know that I care for it much myself, but it's gospel—What I saw looked for all the world like somebody in a long brown habit, like those old monks used to wear."

CHAPTER 6

HISTORY HAD repeated itself with phenomenal exactitude. The position of the prone body was a copy of Gerry Bracewell's position when found, one hand crumpled at the foot of the door as though it had slipped down from the sanctuary ring. The second absentee from the now gap-toothed border of white stones along the edge of the grass had been dropped in almost identically the same place as the first. Under the unconscious man lay a large torch, glass and bulb broken, instead of a battered briefcase. By all appearances he had been examining the door at close quarters when he had been hit from behind. It was certainly proving very unhealthy to show too much interest in that door.

The bald skull was lacerated and bleeding, but Brian had made no mistake; the man was alive. The doctor, kneeling over him while the ambulance attendants stood by with stretcher and blankets, pronounced it as his opinion that the victim was in no danger of dying, and that the attack must have been made only very recently, which confirmed Brian's story of interrupting it at the crucial moment, and suggested both to George and Sergeant Moon, though neither of them said a word, that the boy's arrival had in fact prevented the completion of this duplication of death. The victim laid out helplessly, the stone coolly positioned for the second and final blow, and suddenly Brian running across the road from the vicarage, an apparition in black P.V.C. He might look like one of Cocteau's demons, but he had been a guardian angel to this harmless, intrusive crank whose name, according to the papers he had on him, was Herbert Charles Bristow.

Unless, of course, George thought, unobtrusively studying Brian's interested, impassive face, unless Brian himself had been the one who picked up the stone and laid out the inquisitive stranger at the foot of the door. No apparent reason why he should, but then there were no apparent reasons as yet why anyone should. A cool young card, this boy, and the timing would fit perfectly, in addition to the great convenience of not having to believe, in that case, in the elusive figure of someone in a long brown coat or robe, like a monk, who had vanished at speed among the trees. But if Brian had both provided the tableau and instantly reported it, then there had been no intention to murder, but only to remove the intruder from the scene without being identified.

Concussion, probably fairly bad, the doctor said. Don't expect to get anything much out of him for two or three days, and don't expect him to know much about whoever hit him even when he is coherent again. That was fairly obvious advice. Nothing was more certain than that the victim's attention had been concentrated avidly on what he was examining, and the victim's back solidly turned on the world. If he had heard steps and turned, even at the last moment, the blow would not have been positioned so accurately at the very back of his head.

It had stopped raining soon after two o'clock, so on the paths, and especially in the places where the gravel had worn thin and mud had gathered, there might be a chance of discovering the most recent footprints. But the wet grass would show them nothing, and according to Brian the assailant had fled among the trees and so to the rear of the church, which meant grass most of the way. They would have to go over every inch. He might have left some trace behind. Trees in the dark are scratchy, aggressive beings, retaining stray threads and bits of wool pile never missed by their owners. There was a whole day of the finicky, meticulous work policemen hate most in store for them; and the day, heaven help them, was Sunday. You can't keep a church congregation from pursuing its Christian rites on the sabbath day, not even for the sake of a murder investigation. But with the vicar's help they might be confined to one approach.

They lifted the injured man carefully, swathed him in blankets and carried him away to the ambulance. The doctor took his car and followed his patient. The stone was shrouded in polythene and dispatched, with the broken torch, to the forensic laboratory. The plainclothes and uniformed men available dispersed to patrol the entire surroundings of the church. And in the temporary office in the vicarage Dave and Brian put their evidence formally on record. Until then there had been no time for the finer details, but they were sure of their times, and they had their statements clear in their minds.

"He must have heard me coming through with the bike," Brian said, and was momentarily disconcerted by his own words, and stopped short.

"That's the under-statement of the year," confirmed Sergeant Moon emphatically. "He must have if he wasn't stone-deaf."

"What I mean," persisted Brian sturdily, "is that anybody who lives around here *knows* my bike, they'd know that about two or three minutes after the racket stopped—no, it takes longer than that, I always switch off and bring her in quietly on account of the Rev.—say more like five or six minutes after—I should be walking across home. Not always through the churchyard, sometimes I go round, but still I should be somewhere around, and *might* see something.''

''You have a distinct point there,'' said George with interest. ''So you think this was somebody who *didn't* know the habits of everybody around here. Somebody who might even think you'd driven straight through.''

''Or else somebody very cool,'' said Brian, feeling his way visibly with every word. ''Because, you see, it was raining, and I must have taken less time than usual over putting the bike away. I shoved her in the vicarage shed, where he lets me keep her, and ran for it as soon as I'd locked the door. Really ran, all down the drive and across the road and up the path, to get round to the lodge by the south porch. I reckon I cut at least two and a half minutes off the course. Maybe he was counting on these two and a half minutes, and didn't have them. Maybe he'd forgotten about me until he heard me go rocketing through, and then he thought, all right, what does it matter, I know that chap's timing to the second. Only this time he didn't. Maybe he took a shade too long over hitting him again, and all of a sudden I was pelting up the path like a greyhound, and he had to cut his losses and drop his rock and get out. Either it's somebody who doesn't know at all,'' said Brian with great care, ''or somebody who knows absolutely, to the minute. Somebody right inside, or right outside.''

''And then, of course,'' said Sergeant Moon amiably, ''that still leaves one more person—you, laddie.''

''Yeah,'' agreed Brian, gazing back at him steadily and not visibly disturbed by the suggestion, ''I thought of that, too. I suppose I could have. There's nothing I can say about that, except that I didn't. I didn't even know he was there. Sure I could have picked up the stone and bashed him, and then dropped it and run back to the garage and knocked up Dave—only I'm not green enough to suppose that would give me an alibi, so if I *had* knocked him out I should just have gone home and said nothing. Dad would probably have been the one to find him, this being Sunday. Also he'd probably have been dead, after a night out in the rain and cold.''

"I'm doing you the favour of supposing that you never wanted him dead," said Sergeant Moon reasonably.

"If I was desperate enough to want him knocked flat, I'd be desperate enough to prefer him dead rather than talking," pointed out Brian, and smiled, a genuine if rather cagey smile.

The sergeant, unruffled, cast a glance at George. "You want him any more, sir?"

"This figure you saw," said George thoughtfully, "could it possibly have been a woman?"

The boy, so little capable of surprise in other directions, was ingenuously astonished by this, a thought which had never for a moment occurred to him. Belligerent modern as he was, he had delightfully old-world ideas about women. He thought about it, and visibly the very possibility disturbed him. George put away for good the suspicion that there had been no elusive brown figure, and with it the faint reserve he might otherwise have felt about Brian himself.

"In a maxi, you mean?" He didn't want to admit the idea at all. The broad, fair brow sweated for the first time. "I suppose it *could* have been, but honestly I don't think so. She'd have to be as big as a man—I mean, well, lots of women are as big as *some* men, but this one—it's hard to judge, but I'd say going on six feet if not over. Quite as tall as me. I wish now I'd gone after him, but there was this chap lying there, and I had to find out how bad he was, and do something about him . . . ''

"All right," said George mildly, "I think that's all, thanks, Brian. You can push off to bed now."

"Oh, and one thing," supplemented Sergeant Moon pleasantly, "not a word about monks, brown robes and elusive figures. Not that it'll make a blind bit of difference, they'll be on to it before morning anyhow, but do me a favour, don't *you* set it going."

"No, sergeant," said Brian with unusual serenity and complacency, "I won't."

He departed, drained but satisfied. Looking back, he tried to fault his own performance, but not too enthusiastically, and wasn't sure whether he could or not. These proficiency tests crop up at the most unexpected moments; you rise to them or you don't. He had no special feeling of having fouled this one, as he crawled into bed and fell asleep.

"I just wanted to mention," said Dave, "though you probably know it already, that apparently all the regulars in the bar of the 'Duck' were putting on their usual performance last night for this poor soul who got laid out. I wasn't there myself, but Dinah told me. Eb Jennings was prophesying doom, and Saul was being the scoffer this time. Nearly everybody was in on the act. I don't know if it may have suggested something to somebody—a joke that turned sour. I just mention it."

"Perhaps," George said, "we could have a quiet word with Miss Cressett tomorrow—very discreetly, and get the general tone. We shall have to talk to everyone who was present, eventually, but her account would certainly help us a lot. If a joke was intended, and got out of hand, somebody will co-operate. Thank you for your assistance. I'm sorry to have kept you so long. Good night!"

Good morning would have been more appropriate,

although, this being Sunday, the village appeared to be still fast asleep. But as Sergeant Moon said, as soon as Dave had left them, the word would be going round any moment now that the monks of Mottisham Abbey had struck again.

"The boy won't talk, once he's said he won't," he said with certainty, "but the grapevine will have it before daylight. And by the way, young Brian could have, but didn't. Don't ask me how I know—simply I'd know if he had. In that case I might even have a glimmering why."

"Don't bother about him, he's all right. He wasn't just shocked when I suggested it might be a woman, he was genuinely afraid it might!"

"Hmmm, yes, I did wonder about that. And do you really think it might?" asked Sergeant Moon curiously.

"What, six feet high and a dead shot with a twelve-pound rock? Not a chance in a million! Women have the necessary capacity for malice, all right," said George, "and the cold blood, and every other requisite—but not the accurate aim." He settled down at the table to work out the best deployment of his available manpower for the next twenty-four hours, and only after some minutes of concentration reverted uneasily to his previous pronouncement. "I think!" he said dubiously; and with burgeoning alarm and slightly disoriented faith: "I *hope*!"

"Ha!" snorted Sergeant Moon tolerantly, "where women are concerned, you and young Brian are two for a pair!"

Sunday passed in a semi-daze after the police visit, which was discreetly timed and considerately conducted. They had let Dinah have her sleep out, and Dave catch up with his, and given him time, when he was in circulation again, to acquaint her with what had happened in the night. But all day long she kept saying helplessly: "I can't believe it. I just can't believe it! They didn't mean him any harm, not any of them. You know what they're like, they just close up against the invader, and the more superior he is, the more they make him pay for it. But they never *hurt* anyone!" She said "they" only because she was referring in particular to the inner circle of the community, which was male; what she meant, what she would have said if she had stopped to think more deeply, was "we".

Late in the evening Hugh telephoned, from one of the northern check-points on the circuit.

"I've got five minutes in hand, so I had to call you. Maybe there won't be another chance till the finish. Everything's going fine." He told her, volubly, the clinical details, how the engine was running, how well he was doing on timing, and how few points they'd lost. "How are things with you?"

"Fine," she said mendaciously. "Only it's started raining again now." She was sorry for the police, doggedly parting grass-blade from grass-blade round the churchyard, under the dripping trees. "What's it like up there? Usually it rains far worse than here."

"No, not bad at all. Nothing but an occasional shower all day. Ted sends his love. He's just getting everything possible filled up again with coffee. I'm going to need it before the night's out, but with a bit of luck we're well in the running."

"Take care of yourself. And call me after the finish, just to prove you're in one piece still."

"I will. Be good, girl!"

She came back into the living-room with a carefully bland face, and Dave knew that she hadn't said a word about the night's developments to Hugh. Why

put him off his stroke when he was in the middle of
something dear to his heart?

Sunday night in "The Sitting Duck" was like the
sober phase of a wake. Even the jokes had gone into
black, though they were still present. Eb Jennings
never came in on a Sunday, preferring his pint at
home after all the business of the day was over; and it
was Brian who came to fetch it for him. He stayed
long enough to consume half a pint on his own
account, with his elbows spread comfortably across
the corner of the bar counter.

"Still at it, are they?" asked Saul Trimble.

"No, called it off for the night. What can you do in
the dark?"

"I swear there was more of 'em outside, picking
bits of lint off the trees and scraping crumbs of earth
into pill-boxes, than there was of you lot inside
singing 'Through death's dark vale I fear no ill'."

"He isn't dead," said Brian practically.

"He would have been, from all accounts, if you
hadn't showed up."

Nobbie came and leaned her fair head and im-
pudently pretty face across the bar towards Brian.
"D'you know they've been grilling all of us, everybody who was in last night, about this Bristow fellow?
In case some of the boys set up some sort of a fright for
him in the night. But they never! Well, *you know*,
don't you? It *is* true, isn't it, that you *saw something*?
Go on, do tell us! You know what they're saying?
They're saying when the door was moved back again,
the abbot came with it! It was something like a monk you
saw, wasn't it? Go on, you can tell *me*,' she coaxed,
her voice sinking to a confidential whisper. "I won't
say a word to a soul, honest, if you don't want me
to."

Ellie Crouch materialised as if by magic, and

tapped her daughter smartly on the shoulder. "Come
on, are you serving here or not? Can't you see Mr.
Swayne's waiting for a refill?"

Nobbie withdrew to her duty with a toss of her
blonde head. Brian had always wondered why Mrs.
Crouch had to shove her oar in every time Nobbie
spoke civilly to him. Not that it mattered, because he
was not in the least interested in Nobbie, he thought
her fat and fair, and he liked his girls active and dark.
Still, he wondered what the old lady (Ellie was a year
older than his own mother and nearly as pretty!) had
against a likely lad like him.

"You don't want to let young Brian Jennings get
too familiar with you," said Ellie confidentially to her
daughter, after Brian had departed. "After all, they
haven't solved this affair, have they, and he was in the
middle of it this time, you can't be too careful." Her
conscience pricked; she couldn't really believe that
the police suspected the Jennings boy, any more than
she did, but all means are fair means in a crisis. "You
can do better than a verger's son," she concluded,
again doing herself less than justice, for in fact the
distinct possibilities and attractions of the verger's son
were the chief cause of her disquiet.

"Him?" said Nobbie, astonished. "Oh, *Mom*!
Why, he used to sit next to me nearly all through
school. *Me* go overboard for *Brian*? It'd feel like
necking with me own brother!"

Sometimes Ellie Crouch's family, in their forth-
right innocence, came out with things that made her
blood run cold.

The office telephone rang at about eleven o'clock on
Monday morning, and Dinah went to answer it in the
certainty that it would be Hugh with the final
placings.

"It's too early," Dave warned her. "They won't

have all their sums done for hours yet, and what's the good of reporting a provisional result?''

Dinah came back from the telephone with a thoughtful look on her face, and a small spark of curiosity in her eye as she looked at her brother. ''It's for you. It's a girl. Name of Alix Trent.'' It was a name she had never heard, but she carefully kept the question out of her voice. Dave could not even be sure why he had not told Dinah about Alix; perhaps out of the lingering fear that after all nothing might come of it.

His face gave nothing away as he went to the telephone; but certainly he went with alacrity.

''I know you told me to get in touch with the police,'' said the creamy voice of Alix over the line, without preamble, ''but I needed to confirm something with you first. I couldn't be sure whether to trust my memory or not. It was almost the last thing you said to me on Friday, unless I'm making a mistake. You said 'anything you think of about the door *or the knocker*.' You did say 'knocker', didn't you?''

''Yes, that's right.'' But he couldn't see where she was leading him.

''Good, so I wasn't imagining things. It was the only time you mentioned a knocker, as far as I remember, so I wanted to make sure of my ground before I started anything.''

''You mean you've remembered something odd about the knocker?''

''Very odd,'' agreed Alix. There was one instant of curious and speculative silence on the line. *''There wasn't any knocker!''*

CHAPTER 7

IT WAS the simplest discrepancy possible, and it had never for one moment occurred to him. He couldn't help reacting with: "Are you *sure?*" though the last thing he had intended was to cast any doubts on anything for which Alix vouched with such certainty.

"Absolutely sure. I couldn't tell you any details of the carving now, but I do know it was just a great carved door, with nothing whatever stuck on it, except the big iron latch and lock that fastened it."

"But why?" he wondered blankly. "Why, in that case, should anyone have put a knocker on it now?"

"I can think of one good reason," said Alix sensibly. "It had one originally, which for some reason was taken off, and when they gave the door back to the church they simply restored the knocker, too."

"Yes. That makes sense." But it was plain from the tone of his voice that he was not satisfied. If Bracewell had been mistakenly pursuing a mystery which was no mystery, and a scoop which was no story at all, why should anyone want to kill him? Why knock the second inquisitive stranger on the head? "I can think of one not so good one, too. To hide something queer about that part of the door."

"Yes," she agreed after a startled pause, "that's also possible."

Bracewell had had a camera with him on his second visit, though he had denied carrying one. Everyone knew Brian had found it in the waste dump in the churchyard, minus the film. According to a witness, Bracewell had been photographing details of the oldest carving in the church. Checking whether everything matched, the period, the workmanship, the type of iron, the decorative style? Or if not actually checking on these things for himself, compiling a file of evidence for someone who could?

"You never mentioned to Bracewell about there being no knocker?"

"It never arose. If you hadn't spoken the word I should never have thought about it." And she added reasonably: "But he had his own memories of that trip, he may well have hit on the same point in the end. He went back to investigate on the spot, anyhow."

He had, and look where it got him!

"Alix, the police ought to hear this from you, and as soon as possible. Are you free, if I come along and collect you now?"

"Yes," she said without hesitation. "How soon can you be here?"

"In about an hour and a quarter."

"Good, I'll be waiting."

Opportunity dazzled him, suddenly turning the tragedies of Mottisham bright side out. "And then come home and meet my sister. Have tea with us. You needn't hurry back, need you?"

"No," said Alix, "I needn't hurry back."

It was somewhat after three o'clock that afternoon when Alix and Dave left the temporary police office at the vicarage. Sergeant Moon closed the door upon them reverently, and let out a great breath of mingled wonder, elation and achievement.

"The door! I always said it was the door! As simple as that! Who says we never get any luck? A very nice little witness, that!"

Detective Constable Reynolds, who had taken down Alix's brief and brisk statement at her dictation, and was now watching her furtively through the window out of the corner of his eye, as she walked away with Dave down the vicarage drive, also thought her a very nice little witness, but reflected sadly that she seemed to be already booked. She had certainly tossed a fire-cracker into the workings of the case.

"Well, do we get the thing off?" asked Sergeant Moon practically.

"We do, and right away," said George. "We also get a check on the question of whether it does or doesn't belong where it is." He lifted the telephone and dialled the forensic laboratory. "Your young Crowe is the man of his hands around here, Jack, isn't he? Get hold of him and tell him what the job is, and he'll tell us what tools he wants."

"He's already got all the tools there are," said Sergeant Moon.

"That's the style!" He turned to the telephone as the distant voice hailed him. "Hullo, Joe? George Felse here. Can you get hold of Professor Brazier for me, and get him out here as soon as possible? If he's not available, find me somebody else who knows about ironwork—especially medieval ironwork. And I mean *knows*! Somebody who can date things within a quarter of a century, and locate them by district, school, master, or whatever goes for iron. If he knows as much about stone and wood carving of the same period, all the better. Make it urgent." He cradled the receiver. "Get some of your boys on the gates, Jack, and ward off all witnesses for the present. This is one even the grapevine may miss if nobody actually sees it. This bunch of yours—you know this?—work mainly by intelligent deduction. Sometimes I think we ought to recruit the bar of the 'Duck' *en masse* into the force. But who's to deduce a silly, simple move like taking the knocker off a door?''

It took the expert an hour and a half to get out to Mottisham, but it took Constable Crowe, that solid, silent, deft-handed countryman, just about as long to detach the four heavy bolts that secured the knocker to the door. Their heads were buried among the burgeoning leaves that sprouted from the mane of the mythical beast, and spread out into a round plaque flattened against the oak. Crowe dealt with them one by one, delicately and slowly, reluctant to deface even the black paint with which—surely misguidedly?—they had been coated along with the knocker. Evidence was evidence; and besides, they might find nothing beneath, and be faced with the necessity of restoring what they had displaced. The first minor revelation came when he had removed two of them, and the whole mass of iron submitted to being moved slightly in its place, to reveal a frilled edge of thick, soiled varnish beneath. The knocker had not been disturbed when the door was cleaned. Therefore the knocker had not been restored to its place only when the move to the church was contemplated, and the necessary cleaning begun, but at some previous time and for some other reason. After Alix Trent's visit; yet before the transfer to the National Trust was contemplated.

The third bolt came away with a slight, grating protest, and was laid aside on a sheet of newspaper beside the other two. The beast's head, sanctuary ring and all, could now be turned in a half-circle before it jarred and stuck, and Crowe turned it gently back again.

The fourth bolt was tenacious, but subject to manipulation because it was the last. Crowe withdrew it, laid it beside its fellows, and used both hands reverently to dislodge and lift away the entire weighty

mass of the knocker, beast, ring, leaves and all. It left
the wood with an audible sucking sigh, and he placed
it upon the extended sheet of polythene set to receive
it.

Shoulder-high to a man of medium height, chest-
high to a man a little taller, the irregular, rounded
blot of old varnish darkened like a wen against the
pale, scoured oak. At first glance that blank, un-
cleaned surface appeared to be all they had uncovered; on closer inspection there was one minute
freckle on its smoothness, a little to the left of centre, a
round mole where the glancing light clotted, as
though the varnish had been applied over an oblique
knothole. Only this knothole was not darker, but
faintly paler than the surrounding wood.

"Touched up," said Crowe, and gouged delicately
at the spot. The varnish flaked. He scraped a few
shreds of dry matter into his palm. "Plastic wood.
Somebody filled up—a hole." He didn't want to
name it more exactly, not yet. No one else wasted
words on it, either. It was plain that this had been
done some time before the restoration was under-
taken. "Want me to drill it out?"

"Do that," said George, "and go carefully."

Busy as a terrier at a rat-hole, the drill kicked back
pale, powdery shreds of plastic wood, and buried itself
deeper and deeper into the mass of the door. What
can you hide in a door? George had asked earlier.
And where? There it is, a slab of wood with two sides,
everything about it visible to the naked eye. No, not
quite everything.

In a very short time they had a deep, narrow hole,
disappearing obliquely into more than five inches of
hard, ancient oak, but not emerging on the inner side.
A very minute, staring hole, the significance of which
there was no mistaking. The drill changed its tune,
emitted a brief, indignant whine, and was halted on

the instant. Crowe looked at George, and slowly withdrew the drill in a fine flurry of dust.

"We've got something besides wood in here, sir."

George selected a long, slender screwdriver from among the tools, and probed gingerly down into the tunnel. A faint, metallic scratching jarred through his fingers like an electric shock.

The expert on medieval iron had slipped his car into the vicarage drive unnoticed while they were all concentrating on the job in hand, and been directed to the porch by a lurking constable. He came up behind George silently, a thin, stringy individual with mild, shrewd eyes. They had met before, though not over medieval iron; the whole art of the period was his province, and he had once given judgement on a forged lime-wood Madonna ten inches high, in a very different case.

"What you need, George, my boy," said the expert kindly, "isn't a medievalist, it's a ballistics expert. If that isn't a bullet-hole, then I've never seen one."

"Thank you," said George gravely, "thank you very much. I'd just come to the same conclusion, only I can take it a stage further. This isn't merely a bullet-hole—it's complete with bullet as well."

"To be fair," pronounced Professor Brazier critically, hefting the iron mass in both hands to turn it to the light, "it's a very creditable shot at a match. Even the style of the local carving and ironwork here do appear to be much the same. A layman would never question it. But actually the knocker is at least a hundred years newer than the latch and lock on the door. That needn't preclude the knocker having been made for the door, of course, but in fact this iron can be placed pretty accurately in Sussex, and the possibility of its being made there expressly for use here is negligible. It isn't even likely that it should find its way up here by chance. Nobody'd go far afield for what he wanted, this district had its own smiths, and they knew their business. But I'll tell you something, George—if somebody did hunt round and buy this piece specifically to cover that bullet-hole, then it was somebody who knows his stuff a good deal better than average. And he probably had to hunt a good long time before he found what he was looking for. You might trace it through the antique trade. Somebody must have sold it to him."

"Thanks," said George, "but why go through the entire antique trade? There are thousands of them—there's only one of him."

They had to wait two hours more for the report on the recovered bullet. Sergeant Moon had been dispatched home for a well-earned rest and a brief look at his more regular responsibilities, and it was Detective Sergeant Brice who answered the telephone and handed the receiver across the table. "Here's ballistics on the line, sir."

"Hullo, what have you got for us?"

"It's what *you* had for *us*," corrected the cheerful, enthusiastic voice of the distant expert. "We don't get many fired bullets in that sort of condition. Whoever fired it might have been deep-freezing it for posterity. What did you say it was in?"

"About six inches of medieval oak," said George.

"Yes—splendid! If you were buried in that, George, you'd be there in good condition to hear the crack of doom and bob up fresh as a daisy. Well, this little job ought to penetrate about three inches of soft pine board at fifteen feet, which makes it pretty clear that it was fired from closer than that in this case—say not more than six to eight feet from the door. It's a .25 ACP—6.35 millimetres—and fired from an

automatic pistol. I think it ought to be good enough to
identify the gun, with luck, supposing you ever find
the right one out of the thousands there must be
running around loose with this type of ammo
in—even this long after the war!"

"I take it we're lucky he—or they—didn't just dig
it out and dispose of it on the spot."

"Hell's own job getting it out of that lot. No, if it
had to be covered up, then the knocker was probably
the easiest way, as well as the most thorough. I bet
your boy didn't have any easy work recovering it. But
odd, in a way, going to all that trouble, when you
consider that this little fellow never was guilty of
anything except being fired into a door. No crime
there—except maybe retaining a war souvenir
without any legal right."

"No," agreed George, "no crime there. Yet we've
got a couple of 'em now, murder and attempted
murder, all because people got too inquisitive about
that bit of misdated camouflage. Thanks, anyhow!
Let us have it in writing when you can."

"Right away. So long, George."

George hung up, and sat back in his chair. "All
right, then, that's it. Come on, we'll pick up
Reynolds and make a move. The way things are
developing, it's high time we paid a formal visit on
Robert Macsen-Martel, and took an official look at
that cellar of his."

CHAPTER 8

HE HAD been relying on Dinah to be present and equal to the occasion, as sisters should be when welcoming possible future sisters-in-law, but he had still refrained from telling her any more than that he was fetching a Miss Trent from Birmingham to volunteer some important information to the police, and might—*might!*—be bringing her home for tea later on. Not a word about how important the lady and the occasion were to him. So he could hardly complain when he found no Dinah in the house to greet them. Earlier in the day he had felt that he would need her as a guarantee of his seriousness and respectability; but when it came to the point, Alix and he were so relaxed and so close, after fulfilling their public duty, that they had no need of any third party or any guarantees.

Dinah, as was her habit in such circumstances, had left a note to explain her absence, written on the white card round which a new pair of stockings had once been folded inside its plastic envelope, and propped on the kitchen table, so that he could not miss it when he went to make tea.

"Gone out," she had written unnecessarily. "Robert M.-M. rang up and asked me over to tea. *Very* pressing! Something fishy, or why pick the day Hugh's away? Must go, if only out of curiosity.

Hugh called. Pipped for first place by just two points. Shame!

Dinah."

"Something wrong?" asked Alix, observing the slight frown the note called up.

"Oh—no, not really, I suppose. Unusual, though!" On impulse he gave her the note to read; provided she chose to be, she was already as good as one of the family. "Of course, they did break the ice by asking her over to dinner a few days ago, but that was with Hugh. What can he have to discuss with Dinah that wouldn't have waited until Hugh gets home tomorrow? Unless it's *about* Hugh! And there's no mention of the mother."

"M.-M.—that's this Macsen-Martel family?" She was almost completely in the picture now, she knew who Hugh was, and what were his relations with his mother and brother. "Still, you know, they *are* his people. Maybe the elder brother feels bound to make an effort to be social."

But she knew very well the source of his uneasiness. Suddenly every thread of this murder case seemed to be tracing its way back to the old house where the Macsen-Martels, entrenched and isolated, staved off a changing world. However reluctant he might have been to put his reservations into words, he would very much have preferred that Dinah should not go there alone.

"Excuse me a moment, I'll just find out if she took the Mini."

No, said Jenny Pelsall, looking up from her typewriter in the office, Dinah had chosen to walk. She had left probably no more than a quarter of an hour before Dave's return.

He came back into the kitchen to find Alix making tea. She looked at ease and at home, as though she had already mapped the working outfit in her mind's eye.

"I'm sorry," she said, smiling at him, "I shouldn't take things for granted like this, but it seemed a pity just to let the kettle boil for nothing. Did she take the car?"

"No—walked. It gives me a good excuse to go and call for her, later on, but she hasn't been gone all that long, so I suppose we'd better give them an hour or so. After all, it's broad daylight."

"And still will be in an hour's time, or practically. I'll come with you, if you like, I can be part of your excuse."

"Would you, Alix?" Everything that prolonged her stay confirmed his conviction that in a sense she would never again be leaving. They had tea together in the kitchen, which had certainly not been his original intention. Whatever vicissitudes their relationship might be in for later, it had undoubtedly made the leap into intimacy with a speed and surefootedness in which Dave could hardly believe.

And after tea, when a decent interval had elapsed, they set off to rescue Dinah.

It was cold in the huge drawing-room at the Abbey, and the windows, pinched between heavy curtains faded with long use, brought in too little light, although the day was clear and the time still only late afternoon. But Robert had placed the small tea-table close to the fire, and turned Dinah's chair—the most comfortable in the room, she noticed—considerately towards the warmth. He was a punctilious host; but then, so he would be even to his enemies.

Dinah had put on her most becoming dress, not so much to charm as on the principle of arming herself for battle with every weapon she had. She was even looking forward, with natural curiosity, to the encounter; with even more curiosity now, because there was no sign of the old lady, and the table was clearly prepared only for two. Robert had apologised at once, and with slight embarrassment, for his mother's absence.

"She would have been happy to see you again, I know, but unfortunately—perhaps Hugh may have mentioned it to you?—she has a very bad cold. She's been in bed since yesterday, the doctor is rather worried about her." He accepted Dinah's expressions of concern correctly, and went on to talk of other things, with some constraint but admirable fluency. The guest must not be pestered with family troubles and illnesses.

Everything he did and said, Dinah could have predicted; or so she thought repeatedly through the first half of this tête-à-tête. Of course he would take it for granted that she should preside, and place the tray conveniently to hand for her. Of course he would talk about general subjects until she had nibbled her way through a few minute sandwiches and a scone or two, and enjoyed her first cup of tea. First the social demands must be met, only later can a host talk business with a guest. But there was business to be talked, she sensed it in every meticulous word he spoke, and every nervous but controlled movement he made. A sad, withdrawn, proud, chilly person, she thought, gazing back steadily into his face because he was watching her with such undisguised and earnest concentration. His eyes reminded her of the eyes of certain portraits, trained so unwaveringly upon the observer that the presence of the sitter is palpable, alive inside there, behind the motionless trappings, but unable to get out. Perhaps no longer even wanting to get out.

"Hugh was hoping to win the Mid-Wales this year," she said, making exemplary conversation in her turn when he fell suddenly and intensely silent. "It's a pity—still, he did come in second, and there'll be other years. I suppose events here recently haven't exactly been conducive to concentration, not for any of us. It takes a lot to put Hugh off his stroke, but murder in the village isn't a trifle, and we've all been rather shaken up.''

She had never seen Robert anything but pale, but now it seemed to her that his face had chilled into a clay-like shade of grey. His long fingers moved nervously on the arm of his chair. He leaned to tease the fire into brightness, and drop another meagre log at the back. To escape her glance for a moment? Whatever it was he wanted to say, he was finding great difficulty in embarking upon it.

''Miss Cressett, please don't think that I am interfering in any way . . . I know you'll realise that as Hugh's elder brother I have a natural and permissible interest in his plans and prospects, but I certainly have no right to more than interest. Will you forgive me if I presume to ask you a question? You need not answer it if you don't wish, of course, but I hope you'll feel able to be indulgent towards the liberty I'm taking, simply because I am his brother. I gather that Hugh is—very fond of you. But . . . do you—has he asked you to marry him?''

Her hackles had gone up long before he reached the end of this curious speech, and the only thing that prevented her from diving headlong into prophetic anger on the spot was her acute awareness of the appalling effort this approach had cost him. She felt it in his too intense stillness rather than in any visible excitement. The lines of his mouth had drawn thin and taut, as if in pain, and he was looking at her with what she could only think of as desperation. Out-of-date patricians who find themselves faced with the task of warning off undesirable girls from hoping for marriage with the younger sons of the blood, she thought, ought not to be so sensitive. But could it really be what it sounded like? Surely nobody still existed as behind the times as all that? Living, human fossils!

"We've never discussed ourselves or our affairs in those terms, exactly," she said coolly.

"No, that I can believe, of course. But you must know his feelings, and . . . and your own."

Dinah smiled; for a moment she even wanted to laugh. This sort of thing was absurdly easy, when it came to the point; it was he who was at a disadvantage.

"Is one necessarily always so sure of one's own feelings?" she asked innocently.

He got up suddenly from his chair, and walked away from her to the nearer window. She saw him in profile, tall and thin and straight, quite in control of himself and yet curiously agitated. With his face still turned away from her he said:

"Miss Cressett, you're young and able and modern, and—please let me say it!—very attractive. You have all your life before you. Don't take any step without being absolutely certain of what you're doing. At your age there's no need to be in a hurry, and mistakes are more easily made than rectified. You know Hugh's background. You know what his family is, what its history has been—all those centuries of us . . . The record's there to be read, surely you must know how difficult it would be— how precarious . . . "

She stopped him there, stung out of her complacency. "Really, I think we'd better drop this. Don't say any more, please."

"No, I can't stop now, I must try to make you realise . . . If only I knew how!" he said in a voice that was almost a groan. His hand was gripping the folds of the curtain so hard that a little flurry of dust-motes floated out slowly and uncurled upon the air; she saw them in the cross-light from the window.

"Don't try too hard, because the one thing I've liked about you," said Dinah, bristling, "is that you find this so hard to do."

They were concentrating so furiously upon each other that neither of them heard the soft crunching of gravel under the wheels of a car rolling slowly up the drive.

"I suppose it was your mother who asked you to approach me—though as the head of the household, of course, you must feel pretty strongly yourself, too. What is it you find so unsuitable about me?"

He swung round on her with a face so transfigured by shock and consternation that it was like looking at a new person, suddenly dauntingly alive and acutely vulnerable. But whatever he was about to say remained unsaid; for loud and suddenly the door-bell rang.

The sudden blaze of light in him went out on the instant. He stood for a moment breathing slowly and deeply, himself again, correct and calm.

"Please excuse me, there's no one else here to answer it."

Dinah sat quivering a little with exasperation, rage and amusement, as he went to open the door. Dave's voice, familiar and welcome, advanced into the hall. A girl's voice after it, low-pitched and cool; he'd brought his Miss Trent with him to extricate his sister from the ogre's castle. Not that Dinah felt herself to be any damsel in distress, but after the moment she had just experienced she had to admit that withdrawal was going to be a little more civilised in company. And after all, this was probably the last time she need ever enter this house. She rose from her chair as they all came into the room, and met them with a creditable smile, looking round for her bag and gloves as though the visit had drawn to a perfectly normal conclusion.

"I'm sorry if we're too early," said Dave, "but I knew you hadn't got transport, and I thought we'd better fetch you. Alix won't have too much time to spend with us, and I wanted you to meet her. I'm sure Mr. Macsen-Martel will understand."

"Of course," said Robert, a little stiffly, but not noticeably more so than usually. His manner could never be described as relaxed. "It was very good of Miss Cressett to give me her company at such short notice." He looked at her, and his face was drawn and pale and fastidious as always, the long, straight strands of light-brown hair lying lank and dry on his high forehead. Somewhere behind the fixed, painted eyes the live creature lurked, either in ambush or in prison. Perhaps both at once.

So departure was easy. Robert fetched her coat, but it was Dave who took it from him and held it for her. Alix made a little light conversation about the house and its history. Alix might be a very dependable ally, Dinah thought, appraising her. Then they were all out on the doorstep, and Dave was opening the door of the car for the girls to get into the back seat together.

"Good-bye, Mr. Macsen-Martel!" No need to give him her hand; she was glad about that.

"Good-bye, Miss Cressett!"

They were back where they had started from, with the difference that he wouldn't dare try that again. The door closed upon them, Dave got into the driving-seat; the car circled the island of flower-beds and moved away down the drive. Robert stood for a moment where they had left him, and then turned and went back into the house.

"You did come just a little too early, as a matter of fact," she said, stretching in the back seat with a sigh of relief. "He never really got started on what he wanted to say, but by all the signs his job was to put me off marrying Hugh. Put me off or pay me off—he never got as far as offering me money, I really do wonder if he would have! Who do they think they are, with their ridiculous anaemic faces and their feeble blue blood? In this day and age, I ask you! Hugh will be *furious*! At least, he would, only I haven't the faintest intention of ever telling him."

"He's not the only one," said Dave grimly from the driving seat, "who's got a right to be furious."

"But that's nothing, you should hear how his mother says '*in trade*'—about *you*, love! She's the one who gave Robert the job of getting rid of me, of course, to do him justice he wasn't all that happy about it. She kept out of the way. Said to be ill in bed and under the doctor, but I suspect it's a diplomatic illness." Dinah was simmering down somewhat more slowly than she had expected of herself; was it possible that she could be really upset about such an absurd interview?

In the narrow gateway, which it was necessary to approach with great care from either direction, they came nose to nose with another car turning slowly in. A police car, with three men in plain clothes aboard. Both cars halted politely, as if in neighbourly conversation. The police car began to back out and clear the gate, and then as abruptly stopped; a window was rolled down, and George Felse leaned out.

"Mr. Cressett?—I thought I knew the car!" The door opened, and George came loping alongside. "Have you still got Miss Trent with you?" It was not yet dusk, but there between the overgrown trees a green twilight hung, obscuring colours and outlines.

"I'm here," said Alix, lowering the window.

"If your friends wouldn't mind waiting a quarter of an hour or so, Miss Trent, will you come back with me to the house? I'm going to have a look at the cellar where the church door used to hang, and I'd be very grateful if you'd come with me and see if you notice anything—anything at all—to remark on.''

Alix began to say: "But wouldn't Mr. Macsen-Martel be more . . . " but she let the sentence die away on her lips. "Yes, I see," she said. Until that moment it had not been clear to her that she was the only remaining witness, on this particular subject, who could be regarded as disinterested. Robert's role was not yet clear, and no doubt he would be expected to co-operate, too; but that tall, thin figure of his was beginning to cast a long shadow. "Yes, I'll come, of course," she said, and got out of the car.

"I'll back up under the trees there, where there's room to pass," said Dave, "and let you through. We'll wait, Alix."

The police car slid by, long and dark, and rolled to rest in front of the doorway of the house. And correct and impenetrable as ever, Robert opened the door to them.

"Good evening," said George. "You remember me? Chief Inspector Felse—I'm in charge of the inquiry into this murder case, I had occasion to call and see you some days ago, the day the body was discovered, in fact. I wonder if you can give me ten minutes or so of your time, just long enough to show me the site where the door used to hang before you gave it back to the church. Oh, by the way, I believe you and Miss Trent have already met. Miss Trent did a feature article on the house a few years ago, and remembers the wine-cellar as it was then. I was lucky enough to meet her and her friends in your gateway, and I took the liberty of asking her to come back with me. I hope we don't come too inconveniently?"

His voice was cool, neutral and disarming. And if Robert was going to inquire about a search warrant, he would have to do so now, and in doing so surrender altogether too much of the cramped room he had for manoeuvring. But Robert's face remained impassive, apart from the faintest air of distaste and weariness, and he looked at them without apparent disquiet, and stepped back from the doorway courteously to allow them in.

"Of course not. I realise the extreme pressures there must be on your time, Chief Inspector. Mine is very much less valuable. Please come in, Miss Trent. I didn't know you'd seen the Abbey before. I should have been glad to show you the house if I'd realised, though I'm afraid we haven't always been able to maintain it as we should have liked. In the future I hope it will be possible to look after it properly."

He closed the outer door, and they stood in the chill, dusky hall. The arched window at the far end of the room shimmered greenly with the movement of leaves, in the rising wind of the October evening. It gave almost the appearance of a french door opening on to the garden, but when they drew nearer Alix saw that outside the glass the ground fell away, so that this floor was six feet or so above the level of the sloping lawn below. The cellars beneath this rear part of the house were only partially buried.

"This way," said Robert, and turned left beside the window, where two massive stone newel posts jutted, and a broad, open stairway descended some eleven or twelve feet into a flagged passage, too wide, perhaps, to be truly a passage, more of a square lobby. They could see only a part of the paved floor from the head of the stairs; and across the grey surface, more dimly than here above, the restless shimmer of light and shadow ran like the movement of a brook from right to left. Somewhere on the right there was a window or an open grille above ground-level, through which the light and movement of the outer world could still enter.

"Be careful on the stairs," said Robert scrupulously. "The treads are very worn. Shall I go
first?"

As soon as he switched on a light below, the pattern
of flowing, reflected light from outside the window
paled and submerged into the flat grey stone of the
flooring. The wide treads of the stairs were hollowed
two inches deep, and none of them had ever been
replaced. Alix thought of all the feet that had passed
up and down here over the centuries to achieve that
bended bow of stone at every step. Towards the foot
of the stair they already had a ceiling over their heads,
and at once there was a hollow echo, distant and
delayed, as though someone unseen and unknown
trod always one step behind them. And some eight
feet from the foot of the stairs the new cellar door
came into view, directly facing them.

They stood in a stone box which was almost a
perfect cube, except that the ceiling over their heads
was a shallow vault instead of flat. In the wall on their
right the expected lunette of window—she remembered it now—began at ground level, five feet
above the floor on which they stood, and arched to the
ceiling, but all it let in now, in competition with the
single electric bulb within, was a green dusk rapidly
deepening into darkness. Otherwise this small
anteroom was empty and bare; and the door facing
them was merely a plain new door, a lightweight
compared with the one it had replaced, finished in
natural oak but of ordinary thickness and without
ornament.

"Not as spectacular as the other one," said Robert
with detached appraisal, "but more in keeping with
our circumstances, perhaps. It isn't locked, if you
want to go inside."

He pressed the plain, respectable iron latch and
pushed the door open, standing back to let them go

in. The door swung smoothly, and brought them into a narrow, barrel-vaulted cellar which must surely be the oldest remaining fragment of the Abbey. A low stone settle was built along one wall, and here and there on the wall itself they could trace the round marks left by the rim of large wine-casks. The opposite wall was built off by buttress-like excrescences into three empty compartments. The whole room was bare, clean and cold, and there was nothing in it to be recorded by the mind or the eye.

Except, perhaps, the slight irregularity of the flag-stones inside the doorway, and the shallow, rounded scars that marked some of them. Broken arcs of three concentric circles, centring on the hinges of the door. The outside one of the three was the most noticeable, and reappeared three times on the arc described by the outer edge of the door, which was so wide that it spanned nearly half the cellar when it was opened. Some of the stones were unmarked, some rose slightly higher and carried the scars. The two inner circles showed only here and there, and more shallowly. Not from this door, so much was certain; it swung above the marks without grazing anywhere. Perhaps the old one had dropped a little before it was moved. But was that likely, after all those centuries? And the scrape-marks, though not brand-new, were notably paler grey than the rest of the stone, like slate-pencil marks on slate.

"You remember it like this?" George asked casually.

"It's some time ago," Alix said, "but I do remember it, now that I see it again. I remember the vault—actually it's rather a nice one, and not very usual—and the size of the flags."

Robert stood courteously holding the door wide, not following them within; a gentle indication that

though he was willing to co-operate fully, nevertheless even his time had its value, if only to him. His
pale face was quite motionless.

"Thank you," said George, "I think that's all, just
for the moment. But I would like a word with you
still, if you wouldn't mind waiting until I take Miss
Trent back to her friends. You may be able to help me
over one or two matters."

Robert's enervated voice said with resignation, but
still with immaculate politeness: "Certainly, I'm at
your disposal."

They climbed the steps, and Robert switched out
the light. The arched window showed a clinging,
gossamer darkness of trees, dappled irregularly with
the pallor of the sky showing through. The hall was
ill-lit and hollow-sounding, a desolation. At the front
door Robert said good-bye to Alix distantly, and
withdrew again into the house, pointedly leaving the
door ajar. In the waiting police car, Detective
Constable Reynolds and Detective Sergeant Brice sat
silent, watching the house while not for a moment
appearing to be watching it.

"Well?" said George quietly, as soon as they were
out of earshot in the drive. "Anything to comment
on?"

It was left to her, of course, he was not going to
prompt her, she understood that.

"Yes, something definite, but I don't know if it
means anything. There's the floor—those marks as if
the door dragged. But the door doesn't drag. And
neither did the old one, at least not when I was here
previously, six years ago. It isn't that I remember
whether there were any marks on the floor then or
not," she said carefully. "I think I should have
noticed at the time if there had been, but I doubt if I
should have remembered. But what I do know is that
the old door didn't drag when I came here on that

visit. It was beautifully hung—all that weight and mass, and it swung at a touch.''

''You've got a special reason for being so sure of that?'' asked George curiously.

It was the one thing she had not felt it necessary to include in her statement, but she told him now. They were approaching the parked car, and Dave was standing by the door waiting for her.

''Yes, I have. We were being shown round by the old owner, the one who's dead. I'm told he had a reputation as a woman-chaser. Well, he lived up to it. While Gerry Bracewell was taking some shots of the carving of the door, our host contrived to shut himself and me on the inner side of it—it was quite easy, obligingly drawing it to so that Gerry could operate freely. And so that he could, too. I moved fast, and the door behaved like silk. I remember what a surprise it was to find such a barrier moving so sweetly to let me out. That's how I know.''

''Thank you,'' said George. ''That sounds absolutely reliable, and may be more useful than you know.''

But the look she gave him as they parted, level and long and silent, stayed with him as he turned back towards the house; and it was in his mind that her intelligence worked always one step ahead, and that somewhere within her, whether she had yet worked it out or not, she already possessed the full knowledge of the significance of what she had told him, and had foreseen its consequences.

In the back of the car Dinah said with a sigh: ''I've hardly had time even to say hullo to you yet, Alix, and Dave's only known you a few days, and already we seem to have landed you in more complications than I can add up at this moment, in my confused condition. You won't let it put you off us, will you? Of off this place? We don't always behave like this, sometimes we're more or less normal.''

"Murder's abnormal anywhere," said Alix ruefully. She had told them what had passed in the house, since no one had suggested she should necessarily keep it to herself, and in any case the indications were that it, or its results, would soon be known to everybody. "At least I can't complain that Mottisham is boring, can I?''

"But what on earth does it all *mean*?'' Dinah fretted. "Drag marks under a door aren't so rare, couldn't the old door have dropped a little during the last few years, since you first saw it?''

"After being in position and perfect for centuries," Dave said from the driving seat, "why should it drop suddenly now?''

"If the National Trust are taking the place over," Alix said slowly, thinking it out, "then as soon as the agreement is finally made they'll put their own experts in to see what restorations and renovations are necessary. If a place is going to be shown to the public as a historical monument, then everything possible about it has to be authenticated and documented. Do you suppose that could be the real reason why the door was given back to the church? Not because it once belonged there, but because it would attract too much attention where it was, and might give something away that wasn't supposed to be given away? Is there any real *evidence* that it once belonged to the church porch?''

"Almost everything about the Abbey,'' said Dave, "is an open question. Before it folded, this had become a degenerate and disorderly house. Apparently the standard of scholarship was low, and what was left of the library was burned, and most of the records with it. You could make up what stories you like about the last years of Mottisham Abbey, and if you can't prove 'em, neither can anyone else disprove 'em. The door's obviously a genuine part of the old abbey set-up, but as for where it belonged, who's to say?"

"But Robert Macsen-Martel, apparently, *did* say. He said it came from the south porch."

"He said family tradition said so. Who's going to argue about family tradition—especially against the family?"

"He also said," Dinah pointed out, "that there was this story about the monk and the devil and the sanctuary knocker. But now it seems there wasn't really a knocker on the door at all, not while it was in the house."

"I wonder," said Dave, as they turned into the Comerbourne road, "what would have happened if they *had* left the door in position in the house? The prowling experts would be pretty quick to notice if it dragged, wouldn't they? Old, settled floors and doors don't suddenly change their habits. If that's the oldest part of the house, it would have come within the scope of their brief right away. They'd have wanted to put it right, even if they didn't burn with curiosity to find out how it ever got put wrong. Either re-hang the door, or re-lay the flagstones—one way or the other."

Yes, thought Alix, that's exactly what they'd have done. And now somebody else is surely doing it in their place. But try as she would, she could not see any farther ahead than that, what came next was impenetrable mystery. The question: "Who?" might by now have a potential answer, but the question: "Why?" produced only a blank silence.

Dinah turned and looked back through the rear window towards the overgrown shrubberies and old trees of the Abbey grounds.

"I wonder what the police are doing there now?"

"*They're taking up the cellar floor,*" said Alix.

CHAPTER 9

MOVING IN unobtrusively from Comerbourne without touching the centre of the village, three more police cars had wound their way up the Abbey drive, and found themselves parking space at the rear, in what had once been the stableyard. No one here had owned horses since old Robert broke his neck, and the rank autumn grass was growing high between the cobbles, and the moss shone lime-gold on the roofs. The clock on the stumpy little tower over the entrance had not gone for years; one hand was missing from its dial, and the weathercock that had once crowned it now sagged upside-down against its side. Both time and season had stopped in Mottisham Abbey.

There was one more car visiting that evening, but it contented itself with circling the flower-beds, ready to leave again, and Dr. Braby, scuttling in through the hall with his bag and up the stairs to his patient, never realised that the police were in the house at all. Robert had seen him coming, and excused himself with probable relief but undoubted dignity in order to let him in and escort him upstairs. It was nearly twenty minutes before he came back into the dismal, shadowy drawing-room. Standing in the centre of this mouldering and menacing magnificence, everywhere besieged by the evidences of decay and senility, his pallor and stringiness seemed appropriate, as if he had been sucked dry by his environment long ago, and it was too late now for life to offer him any kind of transfusion.

The doctor's car fussed busily away down the

drive. Robert cast a single glance after the sound, and came back to his duty.

"I'm sorry, I hope now we shan't be interrupted again. My mother is giving us cause for anxiety, but she is sleeping now. You'll forgive me if I go to her occasionally, just to make sure she's still asleep, and needs nothing. At the moment I'm alone in the house with her, you see. It isn't easy to get anyone to come out here for private nursing, but by tomorrow Doctor Braby hopes to find me a night nurse, at any rate. And tomorrow my brother will be back."

"I very much regret," George said gently, "having to trouble you at such a time, and I hope Mrs. Macsen-Martel will be improving by tomorrow. But you'll readily understand that my job doesn't allow of delays, even on the best of grounds. I'll try not to let our presence here touch your mother at all."

Robert did not question the phrase "our presence here" openly, but his thin brows soared towards his pallid hair.

"Thank you, you're very considerate. How can I help you?"

The strangest thing was that there seemed to be no curiosity in him. Tension, yes, interest, yes, wariness, yes, but no curiosity. Everything about this house Robert knows already, thought George, it's merely a question of how much others may know. And the old lady upstairs, doped with antibiotics and rustling on the edge of pneumonia? Was it equally certain that there was not much to be known here that she did not know?

"By giving me *carte blanche*," said George, "to make a complete and thorough search of any part of these premises I feel to be necessary. Notably your wine-cellar, where we were a little while ago."

Something immediate and extreme, though hardly visible, happened to the clay-pale features. They petrified before George's eyes into grey granite, about as durable as anything in the world. The blue-grey eyes were like the inlaid eyes of a late Egyptian bust, brilliant and hard in lapis-lazuli, alabaster, silver, black stone and rock crystal, more alive than life, and yet fixed for ever in one dead stare.

"I'm sorry, but I don't think you have shown the necessity for any such move. What evidence can these premises possibly have to offer concerning a murder that took place somewhere else? I understand it's with that case that you're concerned?"

"The door that has played such a prominent part in the murder and attempted murder with which I'm dealing," George pointed out patiently, "formerly hung in your cellar. I don't regard that as irrelevant. Will you give us permission to investigate as we think fit—on the site?"

He waited, and the stone figure sat motionless, head raised, as if he listened for a faint call from upstairs. He closed his eyes for a moment; the lids were lofty, blue-veined, chiselled into pure, simplified lines like the eyelids of a dead man on a tomb. When he opened his eyes again they were human, defensive and inexpressibly weary.

"I admitted you, Chief Inspector, as a normal visitor. What you propose I regard as abnormal and inadmissible. I understand that I have the right to reserve any such permission as you are demanding—"

"Requesting," George corrected him very gently.

"Requesting, if you prefer. I beg your pardon. I'm sorry, but I can't accommodate you." He rose from his chair; so did George. "Good evening, Chief Inspector!"

"Am I to take it," asked George mildly, "that you insist upon a search warrant? Certainly that's your right. But innocent people often waive it."

"I do require to see a warrant—yes. I think we

should avail ourselves of these safeguards. They were provided for a purpose.''

George reached into his briefcase, and fished out the warrant he had taken out with a magistrate in Sergeant Moon's own proprietary village of Abbot's Bale before mounting this operation. "Very well! I would have liked to have your co-operation freely offered, but you're certainly within your rights. These also are provided for a purpose.'' He held out the warrant before Robert's eyes. ''Please satisfy yourself that everything is in order.''

Robert read, and remained standing for a long while unmoving. The stone ebbed gradually into clay again; his shoulders sagged, the lines of his face dragged downwards into a kind of resigned despondency, and melted and refined still further into a purity of withdrawal such as George could not remember ever seeing before in all his experience. When everything becomes impossible, you go into yourself; you do not necessarily close the door, but you make sure that no one else comes in after you; there is a ban on the entrance, but outward there is still a clear view, even if it has to be upon ruin. And there you sit down and watch, as unwaveringly as a viewer before a compulsive television screen.

''In that case, of course,'' said the remote voice coldly from somewhere within the enclosed place, ''I recognise your authority. I can only protest at what I feel to be an unwarranted intrusion—warrant or no! But of course you must do your duty.''

He sat down. It was more like the folding up of a jointed figure when the human hand is withdrawn. His long fingers gripped the arms of his chair and clung, but all the rest of him was lank and limp in the black leather cushions. Once he looked up at the ceiling, again listening with strained attention; but after that he was quiescent.

"We'll try not to disrupt your existence or your house too much," said George, "and in particular not to disturb your mother in any way."

"Thank you," said the dead voice, "I appreciate that."

George went out to summon his reserves from the stableyard. It was almost dark now, the October evening had settled in clear and still, even the twilight breeze had dropped. A mute and eerie calm closed in upon the Abbey. Two car-loads of police moved quietly through the hall to the cellar stairs. They had picks with them, crowbars, shovels, everything they needed to excavate the floor of the cellar. Robert made no effort to get up and watch their passage or their progress. There was no need; whatever they found, he would be appraised of it all too soon.

After a while he went up to sit with his mother, though her sleep, stertorous and halting as it was, shut him out beyond appeal. At least he could take care of her as long as he was free to do so.

Quarters were cramped inside the cellar by the time they had installed a couple of lights powerful enough for their purpose, and deployed enough men to be able to deal, one by one, with the huge flagstones. This must, George thought, have been merely the private wine-cellar of the abbot's lodging, for it was of no great size. Perhaps at some time other, related chambers, rendered unsafe by decay, had been sealed off, and this one buttressed to continue in service. There must once have been more rooms than this; but this was going to be enough to keep them busy all night.

They numbered the flagstones, and stacked them in order against the wall of the anteroom as they were prised up from their seating. The photographic team recorded the scene at every stage. And what with the concentration of lights and the hard labour in an enclosed space, everyone began to sweat, even in this chilly underground atmosphere.

The soil they uncovered was darkly grey and hard-packed, with seams of reddish gravel. They had begun in the centre of the room, for two good reasons; they had more room to work there, and therefore someone else bent on hiding rather than finding would also have found this the easiest place to begin; and the deepest grooves left by the old door just touched the edges of the stones they chose to displace first. If the door had not dropped, then the stones must have risen. Flags may indeed rise and fall slightly with the vicissitudes of frost and thaw, but in that case they do not wait six hundred years before suddenly heaving themselves high enough to foul a door; and these scars were no more than a few years old. Something more than the seasonal vagaries of the English weather had unsettled this floor. Given time, thought George, it might have re-settled completely; but the evidence left by the door would still have been there, ineradicable.

"What exactly are we looking for?" asked the photographer confidentially, between sessions.

"Anything that shouldn't be there," said George laconically.

Their guess was as good as his, that was the truth of the matter; but the photographer shrugged and withdrew to his work again philosophically under the impression that the C.I. was being cagey. Yet he and everyone else in the group, if required to guess, would have come up with the same answer. What we're looking for, George thought grimly, is a motive; but what we're going to find is a man. What else gets itself buried secretly under a cellar floor? A man—or a woman, of course. The indications were so positive that there was no eluding them; yet they made no sense. They had one murder and one attempted murder on their hands, but nowhere in all this curious affair was there the least suggestion of a person lost, either man or woman. If this piece of the puzzle really existed, it was a piece that fitted in nowhere.

But if it existed, it was here, and they would find it.

It took them some time, but they had the whole night, and could afford to go about it methodically. When they had uncovered the entire centre of the floor, the cross-lights showed an area which seemed to vary slightly in colouring and texture from the surrounding hard-packed soil. They staked it out carefully and began to dig. Eight feet long, approxmately, and five or six feet wide. Big enough. Big enough to receive the thing to be hidden, and for the contortions of whoever had hidden it. The earth grew more friable and workable after the first crust was off. As they removed it, it was piled carefully in the open space against the rear wall, where two sweating constables began to sift it under a strong light for any unforeseen trifles it might disgorge.

The boots of the diggers gradually vanished below soil level, a rectangle of darkness sank into the earth. Picks were discarded after the first foot or so, and the shovel went on steadily hefting out dark clots of earth to add to the growing heap at the back of the room. By midnight they were three feet down, and Constable Barnes had just taken over the shovel. He was one of Sergeant Moon's young men, six feet three of solid countryman, with a light step and a light hand, a serviceable brain and an invaluable gift for looking simple-minded. His sense of touch was extremely sensitive. He drove in the spade, and halted in mid-thrust, refraining from pressing home the stroke.

"Something here—something soft but tough, that gives—Hold on!" He went on his knees, and began to excavate with hands nearly as large as the spade.

Something allowed itself to be coaxed out of the soil, earth crumbling from it as he found an edge and eased it into the light. Fabric, beginning to rot, for his fingers went through the threads when he exerted too much force, but still tough enough to hold together. A button appeared, and as he scraped the soil away, another. When he turned the edge he held, there were fragments and frayed ends of a thinner fabric, a lining.

"Tweed," said Barnes, thumbing the remnants. "There's nobody inside this—look, just thrown in, folded double." He scraped industriously until he got it free, and handed it up out of the trench, gently shaking into recognisable form a man's coat. It was of no colour now but the colour of the earth, but the laboratory would have enough material here to keep them busy for a week.

"It looks as if we're arriving," said George, sitting on his heels at the edge of the grave. "Take it gently from now on, he shouldn't be far below. If a coat had to be disposed of, there could be a hat, as well." The coat had settled one thing. This wasn't one of old Robert's ladies, more importunate and inconvenient than the rest, which had been one of the possibilities in George's mind.

"I went digging with one of the Birmingham University archaeologists, couple of seasons back," said Barnes surprisingly. "He'd have had me brushing away delicately with a little soft paint-brush, just to open up a ruddy post-hole, and here we go digging for real men, not their artifacts, with picks and shovels, and one night to do it in. If you ask me, there's something queer about that lot of values, history or no history." But all the time he was on his knees at one end of the excavated trench, using his great hands, feeling for the strangers in the soil. "Who wants a post-hole, anyhow? When I volunteered, I thought I was going to dig out the foundations of a whole damn' castle before lunch, and the bones of half the garrison after. All I found was a couple of bits of pottery, and a beef bone, and a bit of charred wood. I din' think much of that. I never went again.''

"Is that why you joined the force?'' George asked with genuine interest. The huge, artistic, subtle hands smoothing away the layers of soil had halted, gently probing, quivering like a water-diviner's willow twig.

"Maybe. Live men matter more, I reckon.'' He withdrew his hands for a moment, brushed off loam and flexed his fingers. "Something else here. Not a hat. Not cloth this time. Something hard—listen.'' He had uncovered a small medallion of some flat, dingy surface, hardly distinguishable from the earth surrounding it except by its firm level. He rapped on it with his knuckles, and it gave forth a small, hollow sound, muted by the masses of earth gripping it on all sides. "All right, I reckon the shovel isn't going to hurt this lot much.''

He stood up, and began to slide his spade along the level surface, exposing it gradually from end to end. Dull, clay-coloured leather or imitation leather—the sound suggested the latter, and after all, today's plastics are practically indestructible. Barnes scooped away the earth from round it, and heaved it out of the ground by one end. A large, rigid-framed suitcase, substantial but lightweight, probably fibre-glass.

"Hmmm, all his belongings, too,'' said George. "Shouldn't be much of an identification problem, once we find the owner.''

They hoisted it out with great care and lifted it aside. If there is anything proof against dissolution, terrifyingly enough, it must be plastic matter. Some day we may bury ourselves under a mountain of our own ingenious refuse, imperishable and dead, a cosmic paradox in pastel colours, obscenely mute, naked, textureless and perpetual. And only our computers will survive to record our submersion. In a medieval cellar haunted by centuries of living and dying, the survival qualities of this synthetic creation seemed particularly out of place.

"That's been bought new within the past six or seven years," said Barnes, briefly considering the thing as he handed it out. "That sort of lock hasn't been going much longer. Our Louie bought one something like it when she sailed for Canada to take up a job as a typist, that'd be five years back, or thereabouts. She got married a year after she went there—ask me, that's what they want these girls for. There's a lot of room for a lot of people in Canada." He retired abruptly into his pit. By this time it had become his, he was in sole charge of it. "If I was getting rid of a bloke and his belongings," he said hollowly out of the grave, "I'd put him down the lowest level, too."

Within five minutes more of gentle erosion, using only his hands, he touched something that brought him up short, freezing like a pointer, every nerve taut.

"He's here. This is cloth I'm fingering. Not just clothes—feels like blanket. Somebody wrapped him up. I can feel bone inside the cloth. You'd better find me a brush, sir, something soft, I don't want to break him . . ."

The heat and the rank, earthy smell in the cellar had become unbearable. One young constable had had to withdraw hurriedly, and hadn't come back, small blame to him, and another was looking so green that George found a reason for sending him aloft before he collapsed. In the centre of the minor hell they had created, Barnes sat on his heels, intent and immune, a compassionate man obsessed by his calling, and smoothed away methodically the clinging soil from the folds of a carefully wrapped blanket, now frayed into lace. A long shape, tapering away to the spot just in front of where Barnes crouched and stroked and meditated. With every motion of his hands the swathed body surfaced out of the clinging soil. Not a tall man, not above medium height. Intact enough to yield measurements without trouble, and measurements would show whether the coat could be his coat, the clothes in the suitcase his clothes. And emphatically a man, not a woman; a woman is a different shape, at least until she is merely a bundle of bones, and what was inside this blanket was decidedly more than a skeleton.

"That's it, sir," reported Constable Barnes solicitously. "I can rig a couple of slings under him nicely now, and he'll do fine. I mean, we've got to think about burying him again decent, haven't we? And there'll be relatives to think about—they wouldn't like it if we damaged him, and nor would I."

He ran his hand tentatively beneath the swathed skull, and tender was not too involved and not too personal a word for his touch, and yet his detachment preserved him from passion. George made a note on the most sacred tablet of his mind that he must have Barnes in the plainclothes branch as soon as it could be contrived.

Somewhat after midnight they hoisted out without further damage the body of X, sent for the police van and the pathologist, and settled down to the minute examination of the dead man's belongings. Continuing, at the same time, the laborious sifting of every ounce of soil that had been excavated from his unofficial grave.

The van came to take away the body at half past two. Reece Goodwin, aggrieved at losing a night's sleep but gratified by the bizarre circumstances, had already made a preliminary examination of the remains by that time, carefully unwrapping him from the cocoon of blanket which had preserved him to a remarkable extent. The comparative dryness and coldness of the soil had tended to preserve, also. What they had found was partially a skeleton, partially mummified. The skull was a skull, clothed in dried remnants of flesh but nothing more. The clothes tended to crumble at a touch, and had consequently been touched as little as possible, for they still had, in places, texture and even colour, and the best people to draw conclusions from those were the men at the laboratory. But the shoes, almost immaculate, had challenged observation; almost everything the shoes had to tell they had already surrendered, before he was carefully wrapped up again and whisked away.

The mortuary van drove up as quietly as possible to the door, and bore away the remains with the minimum of noise and fuss. But when George closed the front door very softly and turned back towards the cellar stairs, there was Robert in the doorway of the drawing-room, lean, erect and stiff as stone, staring at him.

"Were you looking for me, Chief Inspector?"

"No, Mr. Macsen-Martel. There'll be no need for me to trouble you any more until morning. I should go to bed if I were you."

He wanted to know, of course, desperately he wanted to know not merely what they had found— presumably he knew that already, since he was here and wide awake—but what it meant to them, what they intended, how they viewed his own position. What he did not want was to ask; and yet a man totally innocent of what lay in the cellars of his house would have asked long ago, and he must know it. Perhaps he had made a mistake in not overflowing with questions when the search was proposed, but it was late and difficult to begin now, all he could do was try to precipitate questioning from the other side. And that he wouldn't do, either, because for some strange reason time meant something to him in this connection, and a part of his mind was surely concentrated even now on conserving every moment he could.

"It would hardly be very easy to sleep, in the circumstances," he said with the fleeting ghost of a smile.

"I understand that, but it would be well to try. There's no reason at all for you to stay up. In the morning I shall have some questions to put to you, probably, but not now."

"You've finished for the moment?" He did not believe it, but it was one more try to extract a grain of information without actually asking for it.

"No, we shall be here. There are routine matters to be taken care of, but I need not trouble you with them at this stage."

For a moment they stood watching each other, both faces polite, controlled and completely closed. Robert was not going to ask, and plainly George was not going to tell him anything.

"I hope Mrs. Macsen-Martel is resting quietly?"

"Thank you, yes—she is asleep."

There was no need to be in any way uneasy about Robert's movements. He never had deserted his family and his family house, and he would not desert it now. Whatever happened, he would be here to face it.

"Good night," said George.

"Good night, Chief Inspector." He drew back into the inexpressibly forlorn nocturnal emptiness of his drawing-room, and quietly closed the door.

CHAPTER 10

INEVITABLY, THE word had gone round before morning. Sergeant Moon had sometimes been known to claim that people in Middlehope passed the news around in their sleep. The gathering pressmen began to be turned back firmly by a patrol car at the drive of the Abbey, and though Middlehope people never collected in a crowd and stared, or never directly, more than usual of them passed by the site, either on the road or above on the hill, and in their oblique way observed and registered everything there was to be seen, and not a few things that could only be guessed at. It became expedient to make an official statement that a body had been found, before it was made unofficially over every counter and bar and garden hedge in Mottisham. George took care of that job early, to get it over and get the press off his back. The information issued was the minimum possible in the circumstances, simply that the body of a man had been found, in undisclosed circumstances but on the Abbey premises, that investigations had been continuing all night and would continue, and that no further statement could yet be issued, pending full examination of the remains. All other questions he quashed for the moment. That was enough for them to know on his authority, however much they—or at least the natives—might add all too accurately on their own.

So now everyone knew; it had reached the stage of being acknowledged, and would soon be in print. The evening paper normally got its first edition into the shops by noon, today they would probably beat that time.

The village had other news to circulate, a curious corollary to the headlines from the Abbey. The doctor had been early at the house again, as everyone knew, for his had been the only non-police vehicle allowed past the gate. What was more, he was expected to pay a second visit after surgery was finished. Not merely bronchitis now, said the village darkly, but pneumonia. And for all her hardihood, the old lady hadn't that much strength to fall back on, it was going to be touch and go.

Jenny Pelsall brought the news to the garage when she came at eight to open the office. It was worse than Dinah had ever dreamed possible. The previous evening had been a forewarning, yes, but not of this. They'll be getting up the floor, Alix had said, and in the dusk and the confusion of her mind of yesterday, Dinah had believed her; but in the security and ordinariness of home it was hard to retain that belief. And now in full daylight, on a surprisingly bright and sunny morning—perhaps too bright to last—the stunning truth appeared monstrously inappropriate and brutal. In particular the old woman's illness, which evidently had not been diplomatic after all.

"And Hugh will be home almost any moment!" she said, almost wishing him away again, somewhere rallying or racing happily at the other side of the country; except that even there the news would reach him as soon as he switched on the car radio, and there it might well fall upon him even more heavily. Here at least he had his own friends, his own interests and even his own home, clear of the shadow of the Abbey and its unaccountable horrors.

"It's lucky he's broken away as far as he has, anyhow," Dave said, reading her mind.

"Yes, I know, but still she *is* his mother, and he's as fond of her as anyone *could* be—I know she doesn't exactly attract affection. And Robert's his brother, whatever he's done . . . Oh, I know he doesn't miss them much and doesn't go near them any oftener than he can help, not when things are normal. But when something like this happens," said Dinah with conviction, "he'll be off there like a shot to back them up, I bet you."

It was a little before ten o'clock when Hugh drove in, with Ted Pelsall grinning beside him, the pair of them in high spirits. There had been no broadcast statement on the case as yet, and they had made no stop on the way, it seemed, so there had been nothing to give them any warning. Hugh sent a blare on the horn re-echoing from the wall as they turned in at speed and drove through into the rear yard. All the nearer half of the village heard it, and pricked up their ears. That would be Hugh coming home. Poor Hugh, what a homecoming!

Dinah had been watching for him, and was out in the yard to meet him as he opened the driver's door and unfolded himself with a spring and a shout. He had an absurd Welsh doll under his arm, a present for her—not the solemn kind, but a randy caricature. His hair was on end, and his face was beaming; if his eyes looked a little tired, that was the only fault she could find with his appearance, and that was excusable, after what had probably been a very short night. She knew him. If she hadn't insisted on his having a night's sleep after his long stint, he would have driven straight back as soon as the results were confirmed; but as she had, he had probably borrowed half the hours of the night to spend with some of the friends and rivals he seldom saw between rallies.

He hugged and kissed her. Dave came out, sober-faced, to join them.

"Didn't bring you the trophy, after all, old boy. Sorry about that, but it was a grand day out, take it all round . . ."

"Hugh," Dinah began urgently, "listen, something's happened here . . ."

The doll was thrust into her arms. "Here you are, love—name of Blodwen. I won her in a raffle at the seediest club I think I've ever been in. Sorry about such a poor showing, Dave, I didn't seem to hit my form until midnight."

"I dropped a couple of points for us, anyhow," Ted owned sadly, "taking him up the wrong track on one of the mountain sections."

"Hugh, will you listen . . . ?"

He began to pick up the story from Ted, as gaily as ever, and then something in their faces reached the steadier part of his intelligence and stuck like a burr. He stopped, looking from Dinah's face to Dave's, and back again; the brightness ebbed out of his smile, leaving it lingering after its significance was lost.

"What's the matter?" he asked wonderingly. "Talk about solemn faces!" He was only puzzled and disquieted as yet, not alarmed. "*What's* happened?"

Dinah told him, briefly, accurately in so far as she had facts to offer him, and without once exclaiming or repeating herself.

"Oh, no!" he said in an almost soundless whisper. His hands slipped down Dinah's arms and held her wrists for a moment, in some kind of private communication. Then he put her hands away from him gently. "But it's crazy! How *could* there be . . . ? They must be out of their minds . . . or else they've put out this statement as a bait, to start something quite different happening—to bust this other case wide open, somehow. That's possible, surely? The other *isn't* possible! How *could* there be a body? Why *should* there be?"

"We don't know, Hugh, nobody knows. All they've said is just that they found it. Everything else is rumour. I suppose the police just possibly *might* give out something that isn't true," Dave said dubiously, "if they thought it would bring the killer into the open, but I don't think it's very likely."

"And Rob's all on his own with that load!" said Hugh. "Mother, on top of everything! I must go to him."

"I'll come with you," said Dinah promptly.

"No, love, you won't! I don't want you in that set-up at all."

"But your mother—I could make myself useful."

"No, let me go and see, first. If we need someone, honestly, I'll come running to you." She saw by his eyes, which had lost their easy brightness and were looking far beyond her, narrowed to confront threatening distances, that he was already a long way from them. So they let him go without protest, and without venturing to offer more help and solidarity than he would allow.

"If there's anything we can do, call us," Dave said.

"I'll do that. But all this is too absurd to stick, I tell you it's crazy. Look, I'd better leave you the Porsche, Ted wants to go over her. Can I take the Mini?"

They would have given him anything he asked, to the limit of what they had, but all he wanted was the loan of the company Mini, which was partly his in any case. He did not stop to eat anything, or to wash, but swerved away to where the little car was stabled, at a purposeful walk which in a moment became a headlong run.

"I'll call you, love!" he yelled at Dinah through the window, and was away out of the yard at speed, and heading for the Abbey.

Robert came down the stairs slowly and wearily after the doctor's car had driven away down the drive. George was waiting for him in the doorway of the drawing-room.

"Is it possible for you to leave Mrs. Macsen-Martel alone for a little while? I quite understand that you must be free to make what ever dispositions are necessary for her care, and I'll curtail our dealings accordingly at this stage, but it's time that you and I had a preliminary interview."

"My mother is asleep again," said Robert. His voice was flat and drained, but he was in complete control of himself. "I'm at your disposal."

"Shall we make use of this room, then? With your permission, of course." Sergeant Collins was already installed in an unobtrusive position beside the window, half screened by the curtains, with his note-book on his knee. Robert sat down in one of the big leather chairs, and George closed the door and came over to face him.

"We've reached a stage when I should like to get some answers from you. But first it's my duty to caution you that you are not obliged to say anything unless you wish to do so. But if you do, what you say may be taken down in writing and given in evidence."

"Does that mean," asked Robert, "that you are going to charge me with something?"

"No, it does not. Not at present, certainly, and not necessarily at any future time, either. The caution is routine even before questioning which may not result in a charge. I have issued it, and you have heard it. You know your rights."

"Yes," he agreed composedly, "I understand."

"By now I believe you must know, like everyone else, the gist of the statement I've issued to the press. But I'll repeat it for your benefit. Under the floor of your wine-cellar we have found the remains of a man's body. The press has not, as a matter of fact, been told *where* we found him, but I am telling you. I am not yet in a position to give more details. You, on the other hand, may be able to tell me a good deal more about him, if you will."

"I'm afraid I can't help you," said Robert. "It's known, of course, that the abbey had rather a bad reputation in its last years, and there are a number of stories of brawls and stabbings among the few brothers left in the community." His voice was so laboured and slow that he might almost have been falling asleep there before George's eyes, and small wonder if he did, for almost certainly he hadn't closed his eyes all night. "Very regrettable, I admit, to find a body on these premises, but perhaps not all that surprising? The house may even be over a part of the old cemetery that was private to the brothers."

"I admire your gallantry, but I hardly think you've accounted adequately for our find. You think he may be a relic of the final disorders of this house in the sixteenth century, do you?"

"It's the first thought that occurs to me," said the weary voice steadily.

"In brown laced shoes, made in Leicester not ten years ago? With a fibre-glass suitcase full of clothes on top of him? Try second thoughts!"

"I can't help you. I'm sorry!"

"Oh, come, you can do better than that. This is *your* house. We have been excavating in *your* cellar. The outside world can hardly break in here to bury its bodies. Very few people have access here."

Silence.

"Do you know who this man is? And how he got here?"

Silence.

"You can do yourself no good by withholding

information, we've recovered sufficient personal possessions to identify him ten times over. It's merely a matter of a few days' work, why not tell us now?''

"I can't help you," said the voice, with carefully husbanded and curiously restored strength, as if George had said something inadvertently encouraging. And maybe he had. A few days, he had said. Maybe a few days was salvation. Or at least the bare hope of salvation.

"We are dealing with a death not many years old, with a man who apparently entered your house bringing a large suitcase of clothes with him, and did not leave again. Are you suggesting that this could happen without your knowledge?''

"I am not suggesting anything. I have nothing to say."

"Then how *do* you account for such a discovery as we have made?''

"I don't account for it. I have nothing to say."

The voice had found a dead level of stoical endurance from which it did not intend to be moved.

"Very well, we'll leave it at that for the moment, but I must ask you not to attempt to leave the house."

Surprised, Robert looked up out of his entrenched and undramatic misery with a sudden gleam of life; he had not expected a respite once the questioning began. "I have no intention of leaving. In any case I couldn't while my mother is in this state. I spoke with my employers yesterday, they will not be expecting me." He said "my employers" quite naturally and simply, like any other clerk obliged to request leave of absence because of family illness.

"Please believe me, I sincerely hope your mother's condition, at least, will soon cease to be any bar to your freedom of movement."

Robert had turned towards the door, but he halted for a moment and looked back; it seemed that he was

about to say something, and by the sudden impulsive
movement of his lips something a little less guarded
and defensive. But after all he swallowed the words
unspoken, and went quietly out of the room.

Sergeant Moon came over to join them at a little
before ten. In the antechamber to the cellar they had
set up trestle tables and rigged their lights for an on-
the-spot examination of suitcase, contents and coat,
before they were passed on to the forensic laboratory.
Within, Constable Barnes and Detective Constable
Reynolds continued to sift the heap of soil doggedly
for further treasures, before consigning it again to the
depths of the trench. But what they already had, as
George saw when the locks of the suitcase had been
sprung and the clammy lid carefully raised, was going
to be more than enough.

The case contained, and in a remarkably good state
of preservation though pulpy to the touch and
smelling of graveyard clay, everything a man would
ordinarily take with him on a journey, a man not
overblessed with money or goods, but still sufficiently
provided, and in fact rather neat in his packing. The
case itself had once been the most imposing item in
the collection; it bore all the marks of its burial, but
singularly few others, no scratches defacing a surface
which was still smooth and dark once the soil was
wiped away.

"New," said Sergeant Moon with admirable
brevity, thumbing earth away from a corner of blue.
"Bought for his last trip."

The clothes, however, were not new. The under-
clothes were mended, the shirts had slightly frayed
collars. Shaving tackle, handkerchiefs, sweaters—
some of the things bore laundry marks, some makers'
tabs.

"Whoever put him there thought that was the last

of him," said George, "or they'd have had all these off. Still . . ." He cast a glance at the impregnable cellar, the massive flags of the floor. "Yes, you can see their point. They'd hardly expect him to get out of there again."

"But no papers," pointed out the sergeant.

There was not a letter, not a personal document of any kind, anywhere in the case.

"Nothing in the coat, either." Nor had there been any wallet in the pockets of the rotting jacket; if there had been any leather or plastic object there, something would still have remained of it. "No, somebody cleaned him out of all identification—the quick ways, anyhow."

George lifted out, layer after layer, the contents of the case, and ran his fingers into the pleated pockets in the back. Nothing there. Well-padded pockets, though. The strong elastication that held the mouths of the compartments closed had still a little spring left in it, and the tough plastic had pulled the cloth lining away from the frame at its outer corners, the adhesive being long ago denatured by damp. Something showed between lining and outer covering, the edge of a wad of paper and a thin rim of black, like the spine of a notebook. George was sliding his finger delicately along the sticky, folded hem of beige cloth to enlarge the opening, when Sergeant Collins leaned down from the hall to announce that Dr. Goodwin was on the line from the hospital mortuary with a preliminary report. George abandoned the suitcase, and went up to take the call.

"I won't go into clinical details now, George, you'll be getting the lot in writing as soon as I can get it to you. But in a nutshell—what you've got here is an adult male about five feet seven tall, rather lightly built, one or two medical points that may help an identification—a finger-bone in his left middle finger broken at some time, probably before he was fully grown. And his teeth are his own, and show some dental work that could be a clincher if you get a lead on his locality and can trace the right dentist. I'd say somewhere in his late thirties—not above forty. How long dead? That's rather a hard one, but at least three years. But the upper limit could be as much as eight or nine. There are contradictory factors—or ambiguous ones, anyhow—there always are in these long-distance cases. I may be able to improve on that estimate, though, when I've finished with him."

"And the cause of death?"

"Your sergeant has it in a neat little pillbox, signed and sealed and headed for ballistics. A bullet in the brain, my boy. Entered through the left temple, probably at close range—a few feet at the most. Looks like a .25 to me, one of the vest pocket jobs."

"Yes," said George, "that sounds right. The first shot missed him and buried itself in the door, the second, fired at shorter range still, took its time and got him. He couldn't get away, not from there. There wasn't any way out—it only looked as if there was."

"Thanks very much for that instalment, George. Tell me the whole thrilling story some time over a bottle."

"Certainly," said George, "if you're paying."

"On my derisory fee?"

Dr. Goodwin rang off with his usual aplomb; and George returned, not elated but encouraged, to his cellar. Sergeant Moon had scrupulously refrained from touching the lining behind the pockets in the case.

"You could have gone ahead," said George, raising the clammy blue lid again. And in answer to Moon's look of inquiry: "He was shot. Seemingly with the same type of cartridge that put the other shot in the door, almost certainly by the same gun and at the same time. He was the reason for the hole in the door, for the floor being taken up and refusing to lie down properly again, for the knocker being put on to cover the hole, and for the door being moved in the hope of avoiding any investigation into why it dragged. A very, very important man. I really wonder why! What made him so important?''

"And how long does Goodwin reckon he's been here?'' asked Sergeant Moon, watching George's probing finger slide into the gap where the adhesive had perished, and ease its way along the back of the pocket.

"Anything from three to eight or nine years, on present estimate. Which could put him right back into old Robert's time, of course . . . ''

Gummily the lining parted from the frame, and now there was no mistaking what the victim had secreted there. Behind the twin pockets were aligned two damp and odorous wads of paper, engraved in steely blue. Not a fortune, but still quite a respectable little nest-egg in five-pound notes. And behind them a thin, dark-blue book with a coat of arms in gilt, and two little oval windows, the upper of which presented them with a still perfectly legible name in a printed hand:

"Mr. T.J. CLAYBOURNE.''

"Well, well!'' said Sergeant Moon reverently. "Somebody who put him here got rid of every direct identification they knew about, but they didn't know about this. Pretty cagey, wasn't he? He had his passport with him, and he had his savings, and it looks as if he was heading for somewhere healthier, only not fast enough.'' He peered curiously at the cover. "L. Issued at Liverpool. Pity passports don't actually carry the owner's address anywhere, but we can soon get it from Liverpool. Better than a dental chart, any day.''

George was carefully parting the bluish pages, spotted with mildew and limper than originally, but still capable of being turned cleanly, and still retaining their text. "Profession! Sales representative. Covers a multitude of sins and virtues both. Place and date of birth: Kirkheal Moor, Lancashire, September 15th, 1931. Height: 5 feet 7½ inches. Description—what do we want with a description, there he is!"

And there he was, in the two by one-and-a-half inch photograph opposite, a small-featured, oval, slightly ferrety face topped with wavy dark hair worn short and parted on the left. Rather startled eyes stared wildly, as usual in passport pictures, but their colour seemed also to be dark, and their setting well-shaped and spacious. George turned the page. "Yes, here we are—the Liverpool stamp. He was alive in February 1965, at any rate. That's when this was issued."

"If we can prove it belongs to our corpse," Brice pointed out diffidently. "Maybe we do need that dental chart, after all."

"Wait a minute, there's something else here inside the back—a newspaper cutting." George slid it out and unfolded it, and Sergeant Moon and Brice leaned close to look over his shoulders. It had been cut from the middle of a page, apparently, for it bore no upper margin, but as soon as Brice set eyes on the clear black type and lay-out he said what they were all thinking: "That's the *Midland Evening Echo*, I'd know that style anywhere."

Spread out carefully before them, limp but intact, was a two-column heading:

"Obituary: MIDSHIRE LANDOWNER AND
SPORTSMAN KILLED IN
HUNTING FIELD."

Someone had found more than a thousand words to say about the deceased, more renowned in his death than in the last twenty years or so of his life, or at least renowned in a different and more printable way. It had not, after all, been possible to celebrate his principal local activities without running the risk of a libel action, but his death had been just as colourful and entailed no such dangers.

The very clear photograph, printed web offset in one column, was unmistakably of Robert Macsen-Martel the older, lean racy and handsome in hunting pink, on top of the ageing horse which had finally broken his neck and its own at an impossible fence on the shoulder of Callow, in February 1965. Only in this· picture horse and man shone glossier and younger than on the day of their death. The widow must have given the editor a photograph at least ten years old.

Hugh arrived with a rush and an outcry just as they all three had their heads together over his father's obituary. They heard voices clashing in the hall above, Hugh's loud and agitated, demanding to know what the hell was going on here, where the intruders were and what they thought they were doing there, anyhow, Robert's low but sharp, ordering him with considerable asperity to keep his voice down, which rather surprisingly he suddenly did. George pocketed the passport and the cutting instantly, and Sergeant Moon flicked the folded coat out of sight under the trestle table, and dropped the lid of the suitcase.

"That's young Hugh home, breathing fire by the sound of it."

"I'd better have a word with him, too, I suppose. Though from all accounts he managed to break away some time ago—small blame to him."

"Hasn't slept in this house oftener than about five

or six times a year, for years now," Sergeant Moon confirmed, "and then only to please the old lady. But blood's thicker than water, seemingly, when it comes to the point."

George ran up the stone steps, and collided with Hugh at the top. A vivid, distressed face, still slightly travel-stained from the drive home, glared into his. The young man's impetuous rush carried them irresistibly a tread or two backwards down the stairs again, and George gave way obligingly and let himself be persuaded. Hugh saw below him the open dark cavern of the cellar doorway, the lights concentrated in one corner, where two men sifted soil patiently into a bucket, and the rectangle of empty blackness cutting between. A look of total shock, blank almost as unconsciousness, dropped like a mask over his face, and melted into scared and agitated humanity again only with painful slowness. He pressed a few steps lower, against the steadying barrier of George's arm, and looked round at the trestle table and its load, the suitcase closed now, the clothes covered with a piece of sheeting. The heavy, chill odour of disturbed earth hung upon the air and stirred sluggishly at every movement. Hugh's nostrils dilated and quivered like those of a high-mettled horse.

"It's true, then," he said. His tone was unexpectedly flat and practical, as though he had shed his excitement, at any rate for the moment with his uncertainty. "They told me you'd issued a statement —is that right?—that you'd found a body somewhere in the house, Rob said you were down here. I couldn't believe it—I still can't. I don't see how it's possible. It has to be some grisly mistake—or else it's a plant . . .'

"By the police, you mean?" George asked mildly.

"No, I didn't mean that—but damn it, even if I

did, please remember that's no more incredible to you
than your version is to me.'' Hugh's eyes flared
again; one of them he had rubbed with fingers lightly
soiled by grease, and unwittingly awarded himself a
black eye which gave him a curiously youthful and
disarming appearance. ''I wish to hell I'd been
here.''

''I wish you had, but it wouldn't have altered
events at all,'' George said reasonably, ''apart from
being a comfort and encouragement to your family, of
course. As for what you call our version, we haven't
one. We're confronted with a series of realities. The
pattern is obscure, and we're not in the habit of
jumping to conclusions too soon.''

''Come off it!'' said Hugh shortly. ''You've
questioned my brother, you've cautioned him,
you've dug up the floors in his house, and you try to
tell me he's not under suspicion of anything? And I
tell you straight, if it's a choice between believing
Robert's done anything wrong, and believing the
police are liars, I know which I'll take. That's another
for your series of realities! But there could be other
people with an interest in planting bodies where they
don't belong . . .''

''Such as the murderer?''

''Or murderers.''

''And entry to this house is so easy?''

''Criminals manage to get in wherever they want to
get in urgently enough, don't they?'' He was arguing
fiercely and intelligently now, but there was something in his eyes all the time that said he was fighting a
rearguard action, and in his heart knew it very well.
''I've heard of houses robbed while the whole damn'
family were gawping at the telly. And *out* of anywhere
they want to urgently enough, too—like prison, for
instance. Don't tell me nobody could ever, in any
circumstances break in here and have the whole night

to himself. Just two people sleeping in the house, and walls a foot thick! And as far as I know that cellar was never locked—there was nothing in it, so nobody went there much . . .''

"Believe it or not," said George patiently, "we even think of things like that. Also of simple possibilities like lost keys being copied, or houses occasionally being let or loaned while the family is away on holiday. And now you're here, maybe you'll be able to help us about things like that. If you'll wait for about ten minutes, upstairs in the drawing-room, one of us will come and join you, and we'll examine the outside possibilities.''

They were all watching him, even the two men inside the cellar, all with closed faces but sympathetic eyes. There was nothing he could do but retreat, since nothing which had been found here could now be cancelled out. He looked with doubt, distaste and apprehension at the draped table and the closed case, and again at the cave of the cellar. He shook his head helplessly and wretchedly.

"You *see* it, and it still isn't credible! I can't get it into my head at all." He frowned abstractedly, and hauled out his handkerchief to wipe from his knuckles the smudge of oil he had just detected there. "Can I go in? I've almost forgotten what it's like—I haven't been in there for years."

"If you want to. Be careful how you go!"

The two constables squatting over the slowly diminishing mound of soil and the sieve looked up momentarily as he came in, and having withdrawn their eyes from the brightness on which they had been concentrating, saw only a tall, dark figure cutting off the light from the doorway, a deeper shadow added to what was already obscurity. He was at the edge of the trench almost before he realised it, and pulled up sharply with a hissing, indrawn breath, recoiling with one hand outstretched for balance until he touched the wall. He stared down into the hole, and George, close behind him in the doorway, felt rather than saw him shivering. When George took him gently by the elbow and turned him again towards the light of day, he yielded to the suggestion docilely, and allowed himself to be steered to the foot of the staircase.

"Take it from me, we don't go to that sort of trouble except with good reason."

"No—I believe you!" He was quaking gently with shock and revulsion, and drawing in deep, hungry breaths of slightly milder, cleaner air. With a foot on the lowest tread of the stairs he turned a grimly thoughtful face:

"Who was he?—this man you found?"

"So far he remains unidentified," said George.

"Well, whoever he is, he *can't* be anything to do with us."

"In that case, time will show as much. Now we'd like your help in a while, but just now we have some loose ends to tie up here. If you'll wait upstairs—Why not go up and see your mother in the meantime?"

Hugh departed, once his mind was made up, as impetuously as he had arrived. They stood listening as his crisp, almost angry footsteps receded along the hall above towards the stairs, changed tone on the broad oak treads, and climbed out of earshot.

"And now," said George briskly, "I want the best roadmap you can find at short notice, Jack, for Lancashire and the north. And Brice, there's a special job for you right here, while I'm away."

CHAPTER 11

IT WAS approaching noon as George drove up the M6, with the map spread on the passenger seat beside him, and Kirkheal Moor heavily underlined, for fear he should never be able to find it again. According to the directories it was a small market town in one of Lancashire's surprising islands of rural peace, shrunken now but still individual between the city complexes; on the map it was printed so small as to be almost invisible. So much the better: perhaps the electoral roll would be modest enough to be easily combed, perhaps the place would be so much of a survival that the postmaster or the vicar would know everyone who lived there, and where to put his finger on him.

He should, no doubt, have borrowed a driver who had been in bed overnight; motorways were not for people who had gone short of sleep. But police resources were never large enough, and there was still a lot to be done at Mottisham; and there were no rested men to spare. George tanked up with coffee, drove fast but steadily, and kept his mind as well as his eyes on the road.

He had consigned the Abbey to Brice's care. Collins would be withdrawing himself and all his accumulated notes to the vicarage office, and if he got through all the conceivable checking and re-checking of reports before evening he would have done well. Brice's squad had still to sift and replace all the soil removed from the floor; and its other main job was the gun. Brice just might have enough manpower to search the whole house for it before night; he had begun already before George left. It was more than dubious whether they found find it, of course, there had been some years to dispose of it, but they must at least make sure it was not in the Abbey. Hugh, questioned as to whether there had ever been a gun in the house, had candidly listed the good sporting guns which had quit the walls one by one as the money ran out, and had had vague recollections that his father had brought back some sort of minor souvenir from North Africa at the end of the war, but had not the least idea what had happened to it—probably that had been sold, too, if it had any cash value—and didn't remember seeing it for years. It was typical of Robert, senior, that he had had a very dashing war record indeed, though too picaresque and irregular to raise him higher than major; and also typical, and one of the better things about him, that he had shed the "major" as soon as he shed his uniform, and refused to acknowledge such a form of address ever after.

As for Robert, junior, careworn and remote, withdrawn for much of the time into his mother's bedroom, he had declined to answer questions about guns as he had declined to answer questions about bodies in the cellar. His eyes and his manner said that he knew everything; but his tongue stated monotonously that he had nothing to say.

So there was George, heading north through Cheshire and thanking God for the motorways which had enabled the police, as well as the criminals, to cover long distances with the minimum of effort; while at the back of his mind lingered the anxieties Sergeant Brice had to deal with in his absence. All the men now on duty in the Abbey had been working without respite for more than twenty-four hours, and would be clocking up several hours more before they could go home and sleep. So we quit the Abbey this evening, George had ordered. Seal the cellar, find the gun if you can, ask any questions that may occur to you, but at the end of the day send the lot of them home to get a proper break. Nobody's going to run, not while the old lady is so ill. And we have enough fresh men to mount a watch on the front and rear approaches to the house, which is all that should be necessary.

In the meantime—he was sweeping past the exit for the Keele service area at the time, and wondering about another coffee and a 'phone call home—there was the ghost of Robert, senior, whispering all the time at his shoulder. People had loved and admired that Robert—not having to live with him, of course, but just seeing him stride across the horizon in his own decorative fashion, safely at a distance. People had also hated him, people who had suffered from him or for him, people who had been forced to come to close quarters, instead of idolising from a distance. What was the truth about him? And why, above all, why should the unknown man from the cellar be carrying, safely secreted with his most precious possessions, a notice of this Midshire squire's death? Clearly this had somehow come to his notice—no great wonder, for the *Echo* covered a third of England and two-thirds of Wales—and had brought him to the Abbey. Plus, don't forget, a substantial sum of money, a large suitcase full of clothes, and a valid passport, brand-new just as Robert, senior, staged his spectacular death. A little man, discreetly on the run with what he had. And showing up at the Abbey in the hope of more? But on what grounds? What hold could an obituary give him over Robert's heirs? And did he know how little there actually was for them to inherit?

It became more and more clear to him, as he pulsed

steadily northwards through the monstrous landscape of the M6, in some stretches of which new bridges produced the only glimpses of beauty, that the date of that obituary—which Sergeant Collins might at this very moment be checking—could not be far removed from the date of T.J. Claybourne's death. There was a direct connection. But what it was he could not conceive.

He stopped at the service station at Knutsford, and called Bunty at home. She was used to waiting around, in so far as one ever gets used to it. She reassured and reinvigorated as she always did, giving little sign of the reassurance for which she herself had been waiting. There is a technique that makes life under these conditions easier, and Bunty had it. She even contrived to provide news that was like a shot in the arm.

"Dominic 'phoned. He's been doing some thinking, apparently. Or perhaps not thinking, only reacting emotionally. He says he wants to go and put in a year at least of voluntary service in India. That's the influence of Kumar and his Swami, of course, but he means it. And he could do worse."

"With a degree like his?"

"Well, that can only be a bonus, can't it? Whatever he does!"

George rang off, astonishingly refreshed. How like Bunty to be able to recall to him a world outside Middlehope, that narrow, deep, archaic cleft in the border hills, in itself a world. Everything advanced or receded into due proportion, in one single world this time. He felt enlarged, and at the same time acutely concentrated on the thing he had in hand.

He called the Abbey. Constable Barnes answered, vast and calm, and called Sergeant Brice to the line.

"I'm glad you made contact," said Brice, expansive with relief. He was young and bright and anxious, grateful for the delegation of responsibility, but even more grateful for continued interest and supervision. "We did find something else—the cap off a gold pencil or pen, I don't know which, but it's gold, an expensive one and not an ultra-modern type, could be as much as ten years back when it was designed. No, not in the soil-heap—in the pit itself."

"Where in the pit?" asked George.

"About amidships, slightly to the left when entering. We've stuck a marker in the place."

"Good, that was wise. Just hold the thing, don't clean it up at all, wrap it and hold it. And I'll tell you what you can do—try it on Robert, see if he recognises it. Don't press him, just notice his reaction, that's all. If you can let any of the squad go before evening, do. I hope to be back in time to make the dispositions for the night myself. And go home yourself when you've got the others clear. If I need to contact you, I'll call you there."

He replaced the receiver and started back to the car, among the hectic comings and going of hundreds of vehicles and thousands of people. Well, well, who would have thought a queer impulse like that would have paid off? What you need in this racket, he thought, clambering in and slamming the door, is lots of patience and lots of slack, to let people run or linger, as they choose, until they trip themselves up in their own cleverness. And their own over-anxiety! Also, of course, a morsel of luck.

But still he did not understand *why*!

He left the M6 at exit number 23, the A580 between Manchester and Liverpool, left that again at Moss Bank and went up into the white roads that veered bleakly towards the moors. He had the impression he always had after using the motorways, of having traversed several kingdoms in the twinkling of an eye, and being astray now in a land where he did not even know the language. And then he was in the uplands, and suddenly it was all familiar, Middlehope all over again, an ingrowing survival from pre-industrial and early-industrial society, an enclosed and private place. And that was Kirkheal Moor.

Clearly it was, technically, a town. It had a distinct centre, with church, open square, market-enclosure and shops. But minute, hardly bigger than a village. There was one new estate, but so small as to indicate in itself the hopelessness of enlargement until one of the surrounding towns reached and engulfed, like a swollen sea, this island of the past. And there were four distinct streets, shooting outwards from the square, and a maze of little lanes and alleyways linking them in every direction. Perhaps six or seven thousand souls in all, counting the outlying farms, the bleak sheep-pastures on the moors that swelled on all sides, even the high mosses where solitary souls cut peat. And all practically within gunshot of Liverpool!

So the end of his journey was incredibly like the beginning. He had made a loop in space-time, and arrived at the very point of his departure. Parking his car in the square, he realised that it could not have been otherwise, that the uncanny relationship was what had made this whole adventure possible, though as yet he did not understand how.

He had luck, for there was only one Claybourne in the local telephone directory. Perhaps the name was not native here. So much the better for him. Possibly even this one would not have possessed a telephone but for being in business in a small way. What he found, in one of the streets radiating from the square, was a little grocery shop with one narrow, crowded window, so stacked up with tins and packets that it was difficult to see between them, and the diminutive interior had to get its light mainly from the glazed door. An overalled girl, lank-haired and indifferent, was wiping out the interior of the glass-topped counter. She looked at George dully when he asked for Mrs. Claybourne, and then turned without a word and went away through the curtained door at the rear of the shop. Mrs. R. Claybourne, the directory entry had said, which argued that there was no Mr. Claybourne, and the business belonged to the lady.

The girl drifted back into the shop, still wordless, followed by a slender, erect dark woman in a black dress and a lilac nylon overall. She must have been well into the sixties, slightly dry and withered now, with grey in the dark, abundant hair, but she brought in with her the instant impact of past beauty. Only afterwards was George aware of other impressions she carried unmistakably about with her: of immense and conscious rectitude, complete self-sufficiency and universal suspicion of everyone else. Not a comfortable woman to live with or work with now, but what she might once have been lingered in the chilly remains of striking good looks.

"I'm Mrs. Claybourne. You wanted to see me?"

"My name is Felse. If you can spare me a quarter of an hour or so of your time, I should be very grateful. It's important."

She studied him in silence for a moment, her fine dark eyes narrowed. Then, without any questions, she opened the house door wide, and said: "Come in!"

He had not expected so prompt an entry, but even less was he expecting the first remark she addressed to him, without preamble, as soon as they were safely shut into her neat front room, among the polished brass and the pot plants insidiously creeping round the walls:

"You're police, aren't you?" Not ashamed, not bitter, just bluntly practical. "Not that you're all that typical, I suppose, but who else could you be? What's he wanted for now?''

"I take it you're referring to your son." There was not much doubt of it; the startled face in the passport photograph bore a certain resemblance to hers, the eyes specially were her signature. "Thomas J. Claybourne.''

''Thomas Jeremiah,'' she said flatly, and sat down in one of the glossily polished chairs. "Tom after his dad, Jeremiah after mine. He was a good man, my dad, church-warden for thirty years, and honest as the day. Many a time I've been right glad he died the year after I got married. Better that than live to know what we were coming down to. But I've got nothing to hide, and never have had. Them that will go to the devil must go alone, I'll abide the same as I always have, in my dad's way. So don't think I'm ever likely to be hiding him here from your kind. What is it he's done this time?''

George sat down opposite her, and drew out the passport from his wallet, and handed it to her, open at the photograph. "Is this a picture of your son? And these details, are they correct?''

She took the little book curiously in her hands, turning it to look at the cover. She had never seen a passport before, much less owned one; she would never in her life have any use for such a flighty thing. "That's him, all right. Well, I never did! I never thought he meant it when he talked about emigrating.''

"He never got as far as that," said George, and felt in his pocket for the one object he had taken from the body itself, a deplorable remnant which had once been a clean, folded handkerchief. The fact of being so neatly and tightly folded inside the lined breast pocket had preserved at least its inner portions, and these had been turned outwards now to conceal the worst, and expose the small initials in Indian ink on the hem, TC. "Can you also identify this as his property? No, don't take it out of the plastic envelope, just look at it."

"Doesn't need much looking," she said firmly. "I marked six of these for him, the last time he was here." She looked up at George. Her eyes were shrewd, and the lines of her face hard as nails; perhaps she had had to be hard to survive. "I always did my duty by him when he chose to remember he was my son. Whether he ever paid his way or not, whether he ever gave a damn for me or not, and whether or not I stopped caring about him, either, when he came I fed him and housed him and mended his clothes. Not for love! Only for duty. He always walked out again as soon as it suited him—as soon as your people quit looking for him and his mates, I shouldn't wonder, but I never asked him anything. When he went, he went. Like his dad before him, who cleared off without a word two years after we were married, and never showed his face here again. I'm not bothered, they're neither of them much loss. I get along best alone. Men who walk out on me I don't follow. This is my place, and here I stay, where I'm independent and respected." She looked down again, narrowly, at the small plastic packet in her steely fingers, and asked in the same uncompromising voice:

"What happened to him? He's dead, isn't he?"

George told her the bare facts. No one was going to be embarrassed by this woman's tears, or feel obliged to try and comfort her. The mention of Midshire and Mottisham clearly meant nothing to her; but she knew her responsibilities.

"You'll be wanting me to identity the body, I suppose. Tomorrow's closing day, I could come down then. And I suppose there'll have to be an inquest before I can get to bury him?'' She knew her duty. There was even something admirable in her acceptance of it, after all affection had been drained away out of her blood.

"I don't think it will be necessary for you to see the body. If you can tell us who his doctor was, and in particular his dentist, the medical evidence will take care of that. But your help would be invaluable in identifying his belongings. And there's money which will probably be reclaimable, and which must be yours unless he had a wife.''

She shrugged, but rather resignedly than coldly. She was not in the least interested in his money. "No, he never married. Too restless, always on the move, job to job and place to place ever since he was eighteen. I gave him money when he needed it. He never came unless he did.''

"Tell me about him. It might help us to find out what he was doing in our part of the country, and who could have killed him.''

"What is there to tell you? I brought him up alone, and I brought him up good, and let me tell you, that isn't easy on your own. But he took after his dad, not after me. Come the time he was seventeen, I never knew where he was, and he'd had three jobs and wrecked the lot. And at eighteen he went off with some smart-aleck friend of his, and I didn't see him for three years. Three or four times your folks came here asking after him, but always when he wasn't here. Whether he did all the things they think he did, I don't know. Far as I know, he only went to gaol once, and that was for some sort of fraud, not a big thing—he got six months. I don't make any secret of it, I'm responsible for my record, not his, and there isn't the man born that can say I've done him out of a farthing. I tend my own garden. He let his run wild. Twice he took money from me, besides what I gave him. I knew that. I never said nothing that was between him and me, and what never touched a soul besides I forgave him. He wasn't cruel or vicious. He wasn't even bad. Only feeble and shiftless and wanting it to come easy.''

As an epitaph, in her passionless voice, it was not so harsh as it might have been; and now her eyes, so dark and full and meant to be sensuous, had a curious measured softness in the unchanged marble hardness of her face. And George thought, if only somebody could have got her out of here, and stirred her deeply enough to make her forget the narrow, cold springs of her own righteousness, what a woman this could have been!

''And when was the last time you saw him?''

''Oh, about five years ago. It was round about the thaw, as I remember, February or March it would be. He came on the quiet, without a word beforehand, like he always did, and after dark, the way I thought he must have been mixed up in something shady and wanting to lie low. But he never told me anything about his affairs. Still, that was the only time he talked about emigrating. Tried to borrow some more money off me, but I hadn't got it to give him, and a gift it would have been, loans to him always were. I don't know, he may just have felt like getting out and starting fresh somewhere else, I can't say it wasn't so. But what I thought was that the police were after him for something, and he needed pretty bad to get out. If I'd had more, I'd have given it. But now you tell me he had money.''

''If he meant to go abroad, he needed all he could get. And he never said anything to you about a place called Mottisham? Or a family named Macsen-Martel? Nothing to indicate why he should go to Midshire at all?''

''I never heard mention in my life of any such

people,'' she said, ''or any such place. He never told
me anything. He was too afraid I might tell the truth
if I was asked.''

It seemed that she had told him everything she
knew, and there was nothing more to be discovered
here, unless through the man's police record. She
would come down by the motorway coach tomorrow,
report at the Comerbourne headquarters address
George had given her, and look without flinching at
the remnants of her son's property, even at his body if
need be; and she would take away the remains, once
the coroner had issued a burial certificate, and station
the sanctity of a notable funeral like a sign of the cross
between her sorry child and his damnation. And
George could believe that she would be victorious.

She was showing him out, with commanding
dignity, when the whole case suddenly opened again
like a miraculous flower blooming by violent stages in
a trick film. From where he had been sitting, his view
had commanded three quarters of the whole room,
but not the section at his back, on the left of the
doorway. As Mrs. Claybourne went to open the door,
she halted briefly and nodded in that direction. There
was a massive china cabinet in the corner there, its
top scattered with home-crocheted lacey doyleys, and
sporting a large wedding-photograph as centre-piece.

"*Him* I blame,'' she said, flashing the first dark fire
George had seen in her. "If *he'd* been different, everything would have been different.''

George followed her burning glance to the
photograph, and felt the short hairs rise like hackles
on his neck. Forty years old if it was a day, that
photograph, with the bride in a big picture hat and
flounced, low-waisted, garden-party dress, the groom
in a dark suit and a silk cravat, and both half-
obscured by the lilies and carnations of the bouquet;
forty years old, but cherished and kept in the shade,

and still unfaded. George went a step or two nearer, to confirm what already needed no confirmation.

The woman was a beauty, cream, roses and jet flushed with joy, without a line of hardness in her face, only a little gawky and a little possessive in the day of her triumph. The man was a different creature, accomplished, exuberant, gay, with a crest of fair hair and a blinding smile. Hardly a photograph of him existed in which he was not laughing, and the laugh was memorable. No wonder even an obituary photograph thirty-five years later had still been recognisable; this was a face that did not change even when it aged.

Mrs. Claybourne's errant husband was identical with that well-known Midshire landowner and sportsman, deceased in the hunting-field, Robert Macsen-Martel, senior.

George swallowed a hasty sandwich and coffee at a pub, and drove back down the M6 in the darkening evening, with all and more than he had come north to find.

No want of motives now, no lack of a link between all these diverse elements.

He had married her! This was the wildest oat of all. Not just a fast affair, like all the rest, not just a back-stairs or coppice seduction, but a cast-iron, unbreakable, unquestionable marriage. George had even gone so far as to confirm it from the church registers, so incredible did it seem. In May 1929, Robert Macsen-Martel had married Rachel Bowman; under a false name, of course, but that did not invalidate the marriage. Mrs. Claybourne and nobody else had been his wife, and Mrs. Claybourne and nobody else was his widow. For this marriage was four years prior to the acknowledged one in Midshire, to his ageing and unattractive cousin with the money, and six years before the birth of the first of his supposedly legitimate sons.

It was a thunderbolt. Why had he done it? Seduce her, yes, inevitably and joyously, but why marry her? He had been younger then, of course, already a roamer and already prodigal with his casual favours. It could even have been when he was in flight from some too importunate Middlehope girl that he had wandered up into these parts under an assumed name, and loitered even after the coast was clear again because of Rachel's bright eyes. But she couldn't have been such a completely new experience to him, why go so far as to marry her? Why get caught? The answer, of course, was there plain to be seen. Rachel had been the one he couldn't get any other way. No marriage, no Rachel. She had had a highly moral upbringing, was as religious as her churchwarden father, and as narrow; and more, she had her affections under control, and was not going to be swept off her moral course by love. Robert had wanted her, what Robert wanted Robert must have, and as quickly as possible, and there was only one way of getting Rachel. She had indeed been remarkably beautiful, maybe he had been genuinely in love at the time. Maybe he had always been genuinely in love—at the time! But there was that streak of ignoble caution even in this act of his—he had been careful to retain the protection of his assumed name, and keep a back door open into his real identity, into which he could escape at need. As he had done, after he had exhausted the possibilities of pleasure with her, and begun to discover the drawbacks. Probably he had never thought of it as a permanent thing at all, just an interlude for which he had to pay slightly more than for most of its kind.

And she, seemingly, had by then begun to discover the drawbacks in him, too, for when he had finally walked quietly out on her she had been relieved, if anything, to be rid of him. Too proud to follow or look for him she might have been, but she had also been too comfortable. Her father had died within the first year of her marriage, the shop was hers, and a better breadwinner than ever Robert had shown signs of being. And above all, unlike her son, she was one of those who have deep roots and do not drag them up merely for an unreliable man.

None of which altered the fact that she had been his legal wife, and was now his legal widow.

And after the wandering husband, the wandering son, taking after his father, coming home when he wanted something, or when he had made some other place too hot to hold him. And just when it was apparently most urgent that he should get out of the country, just when he was trying to borrow or beg more money from his mother to supplement what he had already managed to scrape together, Robert senior broke his neck in the hunting-field, and rated an obituary and a picture in the *Echo*, in an issue which his son happened to see. What a weapon he must have thought he'd acquired. Here was he, prior to those two sons there in Midshire, and there they were just coming into their father's property, ripe and ready to be milked. So he had gone to Mottisham Abbey, armed with his proofs, either to claim his rights or to extort money. In view of his circumstances, probably to extort money to help him overseas. And he had gone unobtrusively, because he was not anxious to be noticed by the police; so unobtrusively that he had been able to vanish without raising a ripple or being missed by a living soul. How could he know how little there was to claim? The obituary made the Abbey sound imposing, the family old, prominent and respected. And in fact wealth is relative, and impoverished though the Macsen-

Martels might be by their own standards, what was left still represented more than many people have to bless themselves with. People have been killed for less —to get it or to keep it.

But there was more to preserve in this case than mere inheritance. He couldn't know into what a hornets' nest he was venturing. All that pride of place and blood, and then suddenly this unthinkably bitter and comic revelation at the end of it, and the boys bastards! A word almost meaningless in these days, yes—but not to such people as Mrs. Macsen-Martel.

Claybourne had said nothing to his mother about his discovery. Why stir up old mud just when what he wanted most was to get quietly away? No, much better leave her in ignorance. George had said nothing to her, either. The first essential now was to get back to Mottisham as fast as possible, and do what was necessary. Explanations could come afterwards.

CHAPTER 12

SERGEANT BRICE withdrew his team from the cellar as soon as the last of the soil had been sieved, leaving it still piled against the rear wall. None had been returned to the trench since the fragment of gold pencil had been found, in case the site of the discovery should be significant. All the finds had now been removed; the flagstones were left propped in the ante-chamber, neatly in order, and the cellar door closed and sealed. So much for that part of the job in hand.

But they had not found the gun.

"There's the old lady's room," said Reynolds. "But we can't touch that, not now. The doctor's been again. She's bad. We can't possibly disturb her."

They had looked everywhere else but there, creeping quietly about the first floor in order not to be heard in the sick-room. Robert, going in and out with the doctor, had passed by them in the corridors as if they did not exist, intent only on his own responsibilities. When he was cornered and made to acknowledge the solidity of Brice, below in the hall after the doctor's car had departed, he was seen to drag himself out of his exclusive preoccupation with a convulsive effort and a shivering shock, like a sleep-walker rudely startled into wakefulness.

"Just one moment, sir—if you wouldn't mind coming in here to the light."

Robert allowed himself to be led into his own drawing-room, and into the slanting afternoon light from the window.

"Do you recognise this, sir?"

The fluted gold cap tapered away to a minute star, and there was a pocket-clip like a scroll fastened to its side. It was individual enough to be recognisable once one knew it, and solid enough to be, in any one house, probably the only one of its kind around. Robert looked at it with his slightly dazed eyes, hollow with wakefulness, and said almost automatically:

"Why, yes, it's mine—but I lost that pencil a long time ago. Where did you find it?"

Brice said nothing; it was not necessary. The words were scarcely spoken when Robert himself, struggling to a plane somewhere nearer full consciousness, knew the answer. True, they had been hunting through the entire house, apart from the room where his mother lay doped and mute and fighting for her life, but not for this, or any trifles like it. There was only one place where such a losable thing, once found, could be of any significance.

The hand Robert had extended to take up the cap faltered, recoiled, swayed in mid-air. Brice, startled, looked up from the hand to the face, saw the abrupt, bluish pallor turn the long features to dead clay, and the eyes roll upwards in their sockets. The tall, thin body began to fold at the joints with infinite slowness, collapsing like a dropped puppet. Everything else had fallen on Robert, and had not felled him, but this tiny thing dropped him as a shot might have done.

Brice cried in alarm: "Here, hold up, sir!" and caught him by the arm; but it was Barnes, huge and imperturbable in the background, a carefully placed witness, who swung a chair forward with monumental presence of mind, caught Robert round the body, and lowered him smoothly into it.

"You think there'd be any brandy around, Mr. Brice?"

Robert drew himself together with a spasmodic effect, heaved a vast breath into his lungs, and opened his eyes. He gripped the arms of the chair resolutely, and drew himself a little more erect.

"Thank you, but I'm all right. I'm sorry, I'm afraid I've been up too long . . . I didn't mean to distress you."

They waited, watching the faint colour return to his face; it was never more than faint, but the livid blue tint subsided slowly, his lips regained a flush of pink. He moistened them, and even that was an effort.

"I'm quite all right now, thank you, I never intended to inhibit you, officer, if you want to charge me . . ."

He waited. Brice remembered the moment for its strangeness, ceremony and civility, all of which were confounding.

"No, sir, at present I've no charge to make."

"But I thought . . . " Robert shook his head, frowning a little. "I don't understand," he said with a deep sigh, and abandoned the effort to find a way through the tangle. And in a moment he tightened his grip on the arms of the chair, drew his languid members together and thrust himself to his feet. Barnes took a step towards him, warily, but he stood quite steadily. "If you've finished with me, then, I'll go back to my mother. You know where to find me if you do need me."

He walked slowly but firmly to the door, and let himself out. In a moment they heard him climbing the stairs.

Hugh drove into the yard at the garage towards six o'clock, and let himself into the house by the back door. Dinah was just beginning her preparations for the evening meal, and had the makings of a salad on the kitchen table, but she put down her knife and pushed the chopping-board away when Hugh came in. She had been half-expecting him all the afternoon.

"Dinah, *would* you come? We don't know who else to ask. Only until night . . . "

"Is she worse?" asked Dinah. "What does the doctor say?"

"He's getting a nurse to come out for nights, but she won't get here until about nine o'clock. We'll be all right tomorrow, old Nurse Taylor—you know, the retired one—she's willing to come in tomorrow, but she couldn't make it today. It's just until nine o'clock, this one night . . . Rob's just about out on his feet, he hasn't closed his eyes for thirty-six hours. And you know me, *I*'m no good . . . "

"Idiot, shut up!" said Dinah bracingly. "Of course I'll come. I'm not much good, either, but it's only a matter of using a bit of nous, that's all."

She made some tea for him, and forced him to eat something before they left; who knew if he'd even thought about such mundane things, in this mood? She talked sense to him, prosaically; he had never demanded poetry of her.

"Now look, she's past seventy . . . nearly seventy-two, isn't it? Don't get to thinking you've somehow *done* this to her, she's seventy-two, and it happens. Do you know how many people over fifty this 'flu's knocked off, the last two years? Well, then . . . "

Dave came in to hang up the workshop keys, and she told him everything. Nobody had to explain to her that Dave didn't want her to go. Nobody had to explain to Dave that she was going, anyhow. They didn't argue about it.

"I'll come round and fetch you at nine, then," said Dave.

"I can bring her back," objected Hugh. "Earlier, if the night nurse shows up before then."

"All right, but if she isn't back by nine I'll come round anyhow."

"I'd better slip across the yard and pick up some more clothes," Hugh said. "It looks as if I shall have to stay over there for a while."

He came down in a few minutes to join Dinah in the yard, carrying a small case, which he tossed into the back seat of the Mini. They sat in silence for a while as he drove out along the lane towards the Abbey. It was nearly dark; the hummock of the rising ridge beyond the village lay limp and quiet like a sleeping lizard. The trees were losing their leaves rapidly now, the next high wind would strip the more exposed branches bare.

"Are *they* still there?" asked Dinah at length. The open gate of the Abbey drive was just coming into sight.

"No, they've packed it in for the day, seemingly. They've closed up the cellar and taken everything away. It's dead quiet in the house now, but I expect they'll be back in the morning. The chief inspector went off just before noon, but his sergeant's been probing all round the place ever since."

"Looking for what, do you think?"

"A gun, I suppose—at least, they've been asking all sorts of questions about whether there ever was a gun in the house, so I take it that's what they're after."

She thought about that for a moment in sombre silence. Bracewell had been battered to death with a stone, the unfortunate psychic researcher, now conscious but still disorientated in hospital at Comerbourne, had also been attacked with a stone. So if the police were looking for a gun, it could only be in connection with the body they had found here in the Abbey. This one must have died by shooting. Dinah had good reason to be able to guess where the body had been found, under the flags of the cellar floor, which had lain level and unmarked when Alix had first seen it, six years ago, and now was scarred from the movement of the door. What could it be the police had found when they removed the knocker from that door, the knocker that Alix said didn't belong there? Oh yes, all Mottisham knew that they had removed it, the grapevine had not been foiled for long! The knocker must have been put there to hide *something*, and whatever the *something* was, it had sent the police hotfoot to the Abbey to continue their investigations on the spot. They had known where to look, and had had a very good idea of what they were looking for. A dead man. A *shot* man. Bullets that killed sometimes passed clean through their victims and lodged in a wall or a tree or the earth beyond. Had this one lodged in the door? That could be one more reason for removing the thing from a site where it betrayed too much, to the safe, calm place in the south porch of the church. But the primary reason, of course, was the way it dragged on the flagstones, and called attention to their irregularity.

"Hugh, I'm so sorry! All this is terrible for you." She would have liked to find something more helpful to say, but what was the use of being optimistic and pretending to believe that a burden like this would simply go away, like a passing illness?

"Terrible for *me*? What do you think it is for Robert? Oh, they haven't charged him, but I know he's expecting them to every moment. They showed him something of his they'd found in the cellar—well, *they* didn't say they'd found it in the cellar, it was Rob who said that—he was sure that's where they'd got it from. The cap off a gold pencil he used to have. They seemed to think it means something pretty grim . . ."

"But *why*? I mean, when we don't even know who

this person was, or anything that could possibly connect him with your brother? Why should he want to . . . What motive can they possibly think he had? And in any case, a cap from a pencil could have been dropped in the cellar any time, it wouldn't mean a thing."

"No, not if it was just on the floor somewhere, of course, but if it was . . . Oh, God, Dinah, I just don't know! I don't know anything! Only that if it was a question of protecting Mother, Rob might do *anything* . . ."

The gravel of the drive, long since more loam than gravel, sputtered dully under the wheels, and they pulled up before the closed door.

When they entered the blue-curtained bedroom on the first floor, Robert was sitting beside his mother's bed. There was a dressing-room *ensuite*, with a single bed in it, ideal, Dinah thought, for the nurse when she came. With the connecting door wide open she would hear every breath from the sick woman's bed. In the main bedroom itself Robert had laid and lit a modest fire, and the glow it gave was light enough to see by. It cast an unusual warmth on his pale, attenuated face, underlined the hypersensitive line of his mouth, and outlined his lofty eyelids with deep shadows. He had one hand cupped behind his mother's pillow, and with the other was holding to her lips a teaspoonful of liquid from the cup he had beside him on a small table. He heard them come, but he did not look up. The old lady appeared to be unconscious, with closed eyes and drawn cheeks, yet when the spoon touched her lips they parted a little, accepting the offered drink.

When the spoon was empty, Robert laid it in the saucer and looked up; his face was reserved, resigned, not troubled by any deep personal tenderness. Only when he met Dinah's eyes did he smile very faintly.

"Brandy and water. He says it can't hurt her now, and may still help her." His voice was low and level, just above the disturbing sibilance of a whisper. He got up and came round the bed towards them. "It was very good of you to come, Dinah. In the circumstances, especially." His eyes held hers; it appeared to be a half-apology for yesterday.

"I'm glad to be some use. You can leave her with me," said Dinah in the same muted tone. "You ought to try and get some sleep."

They left her alone with her patient. Hugh did not go far, she knew, only as far as his own room, a mere hotel room now as far as he was concerned, to empty his case on the bed and strip thankfully for a bath, for she heard the bath running very soon after he had left her. What Robert would do she did not try to guess. How do you sleep when the police are merely waiting at leisure to complete their case against you, and the warrant for your arrest on a charge of murder may be issued at any moment? Poor Robert! Extraordinary Robert, so impregnably patient, distant and proud, the pelican of politeness, the patrician to end patricians! Hugh is right, she thought, in defence of his clan he'd do anything—*anything*! Kill? Well, it would be a kind of duty, wouldn't it? If there was a threat to the Macsen-Martel name and reputation, everything and everybody outside the magic circle would be expendable.

It was very quiet and still in the main bedroom after the men had gone away. The huge silence of the night came down, and she could feel all about her the immense solidity and force of this ancient house, where even the internal walls were a foot thick, and of native stone.

She refilled a hot water bottle and placed it beside the old woman's bony feet, and then for a long time she sat beside the bed, and did no more than record what she felt and saw. The bed was a double one, no doubt the patient's marriage bed long ago. There were no four posts and canopy, yet the frame seemed to have been converted from something belonging to the eighteenth century, broad, bold and sensuous, covered now with faded folkweave, and grinding its castered feet into a threadbare Persian carpet. The fire made the room warm and human, but it must have seemed large, bare and cheerless when the grate was empty. The furniture was on a grand scale, as everywhere in the house, but not outstanding of its kind, only elephantine.

Dinah sat beside the bed and looked at her patient. The old woman's grey hair, unbraided, spread over the pillows in a silvery cloud, unexpectedly beautiful in its gossamer fineness. Against that silken veil the haughty face, elongated still further by the rigidity of unconsciousness, lay staring starkly upwards through large, closed eyelids, thin nostrils spread, thin mouth drawn down in distaste, the very image of Bishop Wolfhart Roth of Augsburg, with the bad smell under his nose. She was a tomb figure already, except that she breathed, and when Dinah put a spoonful of brandy and water to her lips, the lips moved miraculously and she drank. Something inside her functioned still and desired to live, or it would have disdained the means of living.

After a while the grey lips remained still, and ceased to accept what was offered. She had sunk into a slightly deeper sleep, or else into a shallow coma. Her breathing eased and lengthened a little. Dinah sat back and let her alone. Better have a look, perhaps, at the arrangements Robert had made for the nurse's comfort.

The former dressing-room was small by the standards of this barn-like dwelling, with a lower ceiling, and paler walls. The bed was immaculate beneath a candlewick spread, and there were towels laid out, and even a little trough of books installed on top of the chest of drawers. He had left nothing for anyone to do. Unless, perhaps, something could be done about those personal things one tends not to carry on short-term visits because of their bulk. The nurse was coming from Comerbourne, where she probably inhabited a small, centrally-heated flat; she might be none too well-prepared for the bleak chilliness of the Abbey. The travel dressing-gown, for instance, is liable to be a thin nylon housecoat— "because it folds up like a handkerchief". And those thin plastic folding slippers, comfortable enough on a carpeted floor in a new town block, would be like walking barefoot for penance on these flagged floors and bare board corridors. Perhaps something more substantial could be offered, whether she actually needed it or not.

There was obviously only one room in which to look, since there was only one woman resident in the house. Dinah went back into Mrs. Macsen-Martel's room. The old woman had not moved. The sheet over her chest lifted just perceptibly with her shallow, feeble breathing; she was so frail that her body scarcely swelled the cóvers enough to cast a shadow in the firelight.

Cautiously Dinah turned the handle of the large wardrobe that filled one end of the room, and tentatively pulled at the door, which opened easily and silently. The first section was all shelves, most of them half-empty; but beyond that came the central hanging section, smelling of some protective against moths, and of the faded lavender bags that were slung on the hangers. The old woman could have bought nothing new for several years. Everything here was good, solid country stuff, but years out of date; and beneath the hanging garments were arrayed a dozen pairs of

shoes, all old, well-kept, and meant to last, every pair
polished and immaculate, but every pair mended at
least once. Dinah found a pair of sheepskin slippers
with rubber soles. They might well be too big, for the
old lady's tall frame needed feet made to the same
measure, but they would at least be warm. She put
them on one side, and began to look through the coats
and dresses, but the only dressing-gown she found
was of printed silk, no protection against the draughts
from these ancient windows. She stood back and
looked over the array of open shelves again, and a fold
of thick brown woollen cloth caught her eye.

It looked just the kind of material of which winter
dressing-gowns used to be made, though why it
should have been rolled up and pushed to the back of
one of these pigeon-holes was more than she could
guess, when everything else in the wardrobe was kept
with such meticulous care.

She reached in and drew it out, and the moment
they made contact with it her fingers registered a
minor shock of astonishment, for it felt cold and damp
to the touch. She held it up and let it unroll, and it
swung down to brush the floor, hanging crumpled
and stained from her hands. On her it would have
swept the carpet, but it was not a dressing-gown, after
all, it was an ancient camel coat, probably at least
twenty years old. Its skirts, which had been the outer-
most layer of the roll, were dry, but soiled at the hem
with greenish stains, as if from wet and muddy grass.
The shoulders and back were distinctly damp, and the
multiplicity of creases into which the cloth had set
showed that they had been damper still, and for some
considerable time.

Dinah's mind, stung into violent action, reviewed
times, intervals, happenings. A rainy night, an
apparition in brown . . . Could thick cloth like this
stay damp, she wondered, as long as three days? Yes,

rolled up tightly like that and pushed into that narrow
shelf, probably even that long.

There were a few lank, dank threads of autumn
gossamer, fouled with minute fragments of dirt and
dead leaves, on one sleeve. And speared into the
collar she found two narrow dark spines of yew leaves.

She stood there with the coat dangling in her
hands, and suddenly she felt cold from head to foot,
with a chill that seemed to invade her from without,
eating through skin and flesh into her bones.
Sometimes the mind connects too quickly, the body's
energy is used up in a convulsion of awareness. She
seemed to hear her own mental processes at work, like
listening to a tape recording of herself, but with the
inward ear.

Three nights ago, Saturday night, the psychic
research man was knocked on the head. It poured
with rain that night. The grass in the churchyard is
long, and would be very wet. There are yew trees
there. Someone was seen there in a long, brown robe,
like a monk, vanishing among the trees. Someone
who went there knowing there was something that
must not be investigated about that door, and afraid
that the researches would not all be psychic. Then
that same someone knew about the bullet-hole, if it is
a bullet-hole—knew, in any case, about whatever it is
that shouldn't be there and had to be covered up.

Perhaps they had been looking for more than a
gun when they searched the house. But they had not
searched this room. Impossible to intrude upon
mortal illness. There is, after all, only one sure way to
escape consequences, and that is to die. She even
turned back to the bed to look again at the sleeper, to
make sure that this was still sleep. For a moment she
would almost have been willing to believe that even
mortal illness can be induced, when the need is great
enough. But the old woman, austere and still, lay

coldly indifferent to all suspicions, the faint rustling in her chest her only comment.

Dinah slid her hand into the right-hand pocket of the coat she held, and her fingers closed over a small round object. Damp here, too, from a rain-wet hand that had thrust this little thing within. She felt the left-hand pocket, and the lining was dry.

The door opened so quietly behind her that she did not hear it, but the soft steps on the interval of bare boards reached her ears, and she swung round almost guiltily. Hugh had come in on tip-toe, flushed and relaxed from his bath, but gingerly and uneasy in a sickroom, and was looking at her with a surprised smile, because she had started so violently.

"Did I startle you? Sorry!" he whispered. He had dressed fully again, evidently he was prepared to come and sit out the vigil with her, and drive her home as he had promised, if the nurse came in good time. "Whatever have you got there?"

He came nearer, still treading stealthily, still smiling. She wanted to roll up the coat and thrust it away again out of his sight, but it was far too late for such a move. Mutely she let him take it from her. In a whisper she said: "I was looking for a warm dressing-gown—for the nurse . . ."

"Where did you find . . . ?" He broke off there on a sharp, indrawn breath, seeing the wardrobe door open. His hands, suddenly intent, felt at the woollen cloth here and there. One of the yew spines came away and lay in the palm of his hand. He stared at it, and Dinah saw his face tighten and shiver, saw him shake his head and stare again. He, too, could connect, as rapidly as anyone.

In a frightened whisper, barely audible at all, he said: "Oh, *no*! Oh, my God—Mother!"

CHAPTER 13

THEY STOOD staring at each other with wide, horrified eyes across the draggled coat and the brittle, broken leaf. Hugh opened his lips to blurt out something unguarded, a protest, a cry of rejection, an appeal—no, more likely a demand!—for reassurance, but Dinah motioned him urgently to be quiet, and he swallowed his distress and cast one brief, alarmed glance at the bed. It was impossible to talk there. No revelation, however stunning, had a right to intervene in the struggle now on in this room between life and death.

It was the intensity and helplessness of their silence that made it possible for them to hear Robert's footsteps on the stairs. Hugh came out of his stupor with a shudder, rolled up the coat hastily and pushed it to the back of one of the shelves. He had scarcely closed the door upon it when Robert came in.

"I've made you some coffee and sandwiches," he said, in a muted half-voice that was less disturbing than a whisper. "You go down and get them in peace. I'll sit with her while you're away."

"You should be sleeping," said Dinah as quietly.

"Later, when the nurse is here. I've called Doctor Braby again," he said, and looked long and sombrely at the figure in the bed, withdrawn and immune. "I'm worried about her. She doesn't rally. I think he should see her again."

"But really I don't need anything," Dinah began gently. But Hugh's brows were signalling her urgently to accept, to come away out of here where they could talk; and Hugh's hand was persuasive at her elbow, drawing her towards the door. They needed time to consider what it really was they had discovered, to come to terms with what they knew, before anyone else need know it. Yes, she thought, he's right. Why put it off? It won't go away, and it can't be kept secret. We've got to talk. Why not now? She yielded to the coaxing hand that urged her away. "Oh, very well—it's kind of you, Robert, I'll be back very soon."

Hugh closed the bedroom door very softly and cautiously after them. The house crowded in upon them, heavy, ancient and cold, as they crept down the stairs in silence. Dinah had glanced back just once as the door closed, and seen Robert seated again beside his mother's bed, indestructibly patient, lonely and durable; the man who made coffee, filled hot-water bottles, put fresh, aired sheets on the bed for the nurse, brought up books for her to read, thought of everything and did everything that was needed in this house. There might have been a whole generation instead of six years between him and Hugh. Then he was shut in and they were shut out, and the vast treads of the stairs creaked softly under their feet; and she realised that they were hurrying, that they were frantic to reach some enclosed place, with at least one more solid door between themselves and the pair upstairs, where they could turn and look at each other without concealment at last, and say everything they had to say.

Robert had laid a tray as meticulously as for a full-dress party, and placed it on a low round table of Benares brass in the drawing-room, and even plugged in a little electric fire on the vast empty hearth, a spark in a cold cavern. One standard lamp was switched on beside the table; the rest of the room receded into darkness. Hugh closed the door behind them, and leaned back against it with a huge sigh of wonder and dismay.

"My God, Dinah, what are we going to do?"

She didn't answer. She had walked on into the room as soon as he released her arm, moving automatically towards the circle of light in which the table stood, though she had no more thought of coffee at that moment than he had. She even touched the arched handle of the porcelain pot, vaguely, as if she wondered what she was doing here, and could only associate her presence with these small evidences of Robert's scrupulous attention to his guest. Her hand dropped. She looked up at Hugh, still pressed against the door with his arms spread and his head turning tormentedly from side to side.

"It can't be true, can it? *Can* it? That coat—and this cold of hers—the next day she was worse, suddenly much worse . . . You remember how it rained when you drove me over here that night?"

Yes, she remembered. She noted, too, realising it for the first time, that when he spoke of the Abbey he never said "home". Home was the flat over the workshop. Grooms should live above the stables.

"Then she knew everything about it—all the time she knew," he said in a drained whisper. "*Not Robert* . . ."

Dinah gazed back at him large-eyed across the table. "No, not Robert. I should have known."

Hugh heaved himself away from the door, and began to pace helplessly about the room, grinding his heels into the frayed carpet: a few steps away from her, a few steps back again.

"Not Robert—*Mother*! The poor old girl, she must have been *mad*! Dinah, she *must* have been mad, mustn't she? Why should she want to slug a poor harmless crank for hanging round that damned door,

unless she knew what was wrong with it? And if she
knew that, then she knew *why* . . . She must have been
the one who . . . There isn't any other possibility left,
is there? But why? *Why*? Who *was* this fellow they
found, anyhow?''

''I don't know that,'' said Dinah. Her voice
sounded to her curiously distinct and pitched a little
high, as though she stood a long way off, and had to
make it reach not only Hugh, but herself. ''All I know
is who killed him. Not why.''

''Yes . . . there's no escaping that now, is there?''

''And it wasn't Robert,'' she said, with the same
distant, hypnotic authority.

''No, not Robert. So what, for God's sake, are we
going to do now?''

In the moment of silence she heard the ticking of
the clock, and would have liked to know how its hands
stood, but it was shrouded in darkness in a corner of
the room, and in any case she could not turn her eyes
away because of the intensity with which Hugh's eyes
held them.

''*And it wasn't your mother*,'' she said.

For a moment he thought he had not heard her
correctly, though she had incised the words upon the
stillness between them with all the clarity of an
engraving; then he knew that he had, and that she
had meant what she said, and after all his restless and
agonised writhings he was suddenly quite still, intent
and silent while he studied her.

''But that's crazy!'' he said. ''You saw her coat,
still green and damp from being rolled away like that
on Saturday night, all soaked with rain. And stuck
with yew needles—what more could we possibly need
than that? Damn it, Dinah, it was you who found it!''

''Yes, I found it. Does that prove who wore it?
Somebody wore it to steal out to the churchyard, I give

you that. How can we be so sure it was your mother?''

"But, hell, Dinah, you just found it hidden in her room . . ."

"Yes . . . the one place in the house, you tell me, that hasn't been searched. The best place to hide something. I wonder,'' said Dinah, ''if the gun's there, too? She wouldn't know, would she? For two days now she's been either asleep or more or less in a coma. Anybody could have hidden the coat there.''

A gust of incredulous laughter shook him. *"Anybody,* the girl says! For God's sake, how many people were there in the house?''

"There was one extra last Saturday night,'' said Dinah. *"There was you!''*

He took two or three hasty steps towards her, as though he wanted to use his hands, the brusque persuasion of his body, to recall her to herself and put an end to this grotesque nightmare of distrust and misunderstanding. She did not move to meet him, nor to recoil from him, but kept her place, the brass table solidly between them.

"Dinah, you don't know what you're saying. You can't mean this!''

"I know what I'm saying. You slept in this house on Saturday night. I drove you over here, as you just reminded me. Who else belonging to this house knew there was going to be a watcher prying round the church porch all night? Had your mother been in the bar listening? Had Robert? But *you* had! *You* knew! 'If the monks don't get you, the devil will,' you said. And you had a fine monk's robe all waiting for you here by the garden door. You'd be surprised, Hugh,'' she said, ''how many details a girl notices when she's paying her first visit to people who may be going to be her in-laws. I saw the worn rugs in the hall, and the old coats in the lobby. The kind of old coats most houses keep, pensioned off, just for running out in the rain when you've forgotten to shut the garage door— or popping out to feed the chickens, if you keep chickens. I remember that old camel coat very well. It could make a fine monk out of anyone in the dark, man or woman, and it wasn't in your mother's wardrobe then.''

''But, by God, all you're saying is that *any* of us could have put it on. Because I told them all about that fool of a ghost-hunter, when I came in, that night—they may not have been there to hear it for themselves, but they knew, all right. How could I know she'd get up in the small hours and go blundering out there to catch her death?''

She stared steadily into his face, and everything about him seemed to her a kind of charade, expertly played, the warmth of his voice, full of indignant innocence, the hurt anger of his eyes, that could meet hers even now without evasion and without blinking; but all wasted, because she knew the answer before the charade was played.

''And what about her shoes, Hugh? If she went out in the wet grass on Saturday night, where are the shoes she wore? Every pair she had in her wardrobe is dry and polished. Who cleaned them and put them away for her? By the next morning she was too ill to get up.''

He opened his lips to answer that, too, with the same assurance and the same indignation, without a pause, never at a loss; but she raised her voice abruptly, and rode over him.

''No, don't bother to think up any more lies, it wouldn't alter anything. Do you know what I found in the pocket of the coat? It was intelligent of you to pull it off and put it in your pocket, if it was hanging loose, because if it had dropped off in the churchyard they'd have found it, for certain. But you really

should have remembered to take it out when you got
back to the house.''

She leaned towards him across the table, holding it
out on the palm of her hand. A small, plain horn
button, still tethered to a fine green thread, with a few
torn fibres of grey-green wool attached.

''But you didn't think about it, and now you've
missed your chance. And it was bad luck, wasn't it,
that I happened to be the one to find it. The one
person who couldn't fail to know it again. The one
person who could swear you were wearing it last
Saturday night.'' She was vibrating like a taut
bowstring, not with fear or even shock now, but with
the current of knowledge suddenly streaming through
her to earth, things she had always known and never
acknowledged before. ''I knitted the cardigan. I
stitched these buttons on. How many men do I knit
for? I hardly know how to knit, beyond plain and
purl! It was an aberration, even when I did it for
you.''

She hardly knew who this could be, talking with her
voice, through her throat, still quietly but now with a
kind of ferocity of which she had not known she was
capable. But the man facing her she knew, through
and through she knew him, and there was no longer
anything he could say or do that would fool her. He
was still smiling, baffled, hurt, shaking his head over
her, opening his mouth to protest once again, to
breathe sweet reason and blow even this away. And
he could do it better than anyone she had ever known
but never again well enough to take her in.

''No, don't tell me *Robert* borrowed *your* clothes!
Make up your mind which of them you want to
frame, and stick to it! You took whatever you fancied
of *his*, I can see that now, but never the other way
round. Like that gold pencil you were telling me
about—the cap that turned up in the cellar. It hadn't

been there long, had it? Before all this began, about three weeks ago, I remember you signing for a parcel in the office with a gold pencil—that wouldn't be the same one, would it, Hugh? The one Robert lost a long time ago? Did they let you into the cellar where they were digging, Hugh? Mightn't they have done that purposely, just to see what turned up afterwards, where nothing was before? You're not the only clever one! Did you ever think of that?''

He had not. She saw the thought sharpen the brightness of his eyes into the bleak grey of steel, while his appalled, compassionate smile for her unaccountable madness remained fixed.

''Oh, yes, all kinds of things come back to me now. Who escaped from this house and left the others holding the baby? *You did!* Who relied on Robert's determination to protect your mother and keep your name clean? *You did!* Who landed him in this hell and left him to cope with it alone? *You did!* Who's been busy planting evidence to saddle him with the murder, now that it can't be hushed up any longer? *You have!* And who's willing now to switch from his brother to his mother for scapegoat if it looks a better bet? *You are!*''

''Dinah!'' he said, quite softly.

''I don't know who that man was, or why you shot him, but I know you did,'' she said with absolute finality.

''Do you, Dinah? And the photographer, too? And that idiot of a psychic researcher on Saturday night? What, all of them, Dinah?''

''All of them,'' said Dinah.

''Then what makes you think I'll stick off at you?''

She hardly saw the movement of his hand, because she was so intent on his face, which had dropped all its pretence of shock and innocence and vulnerability, and was gazing at her with steady, calculating concentration. This was more like Hugh, the Hugh she had known, who kept no rules but his own, and changed even those to suit his present convenience; Hugh bright, hard, self-centred and resolute. How often in the past she had called him awful, a devil, told him he didn't give a damn for anyone, telling herself, at the same time, the exact truth of what she knew; but what she had always failed to do was to take these truths seriously. Now she knew better. And now he had taken one deliberate step towards the circle of light from the lamp, to let her see the gun in his hand.

"That's one thing you were wrong about, Dinah girl. This wasn't hidden in Mother's room, it was among my shirts, over there at the flat. I picked it up this evening. It's loaded. And Dad and I always kept his little war souvenir in good working fettle. We used to practise at a target in the garden. It doesn't make a very alarming sound, through these walls it wouldn't carry far. But it kills, Dinah."

"Yes," she said, "we know it kills."

Such a tiny thing, blue-black; the barrel jutting out of his fist couldn't have been more than three inches long, and the whole small weapon scarcely six. It was hard to believe in it, harder still to be afraid of it. She might as well have been looking at a toy, and yet she had good reason to know that it could kill. And curiously, it mattered a great deal that she had never had any practice in being afraid. It cannot be learned all in a minute. In particular she had never before had any reason to be afraid of Hugh, and now that she had good reason, she found it difficult to take even this seriously. In theory she believed; in practice, however incredibly, she suddenly laughed aloud. It disconcerted and yet for a moment encouraged him. She had known him, perhaps, better than he had known her.

"Look, Dinah, all I've done is what I had to do, and I'm going through with it, and my God, surely you're not the one to stop me? Hell, you think I don't know you've been fond of me? And I wanted you, and I still want you. Dinah, I'm getting out of here . . . "

"You won't get out," she said. "They'll be watching the gates. They're not as green as you think."

"I'll get out. There are other ways than through the gates. The Porsche's there in the yard at home, they're not watching that. Dinah—*come with me!*"

For one moment she actually thought he meant it. It made no difference, she had already recoiled with so much detestation that no possible tenderness or hope in him could have survived the implications; but for one single instant she almost believed he wanted her to go with him alive. Then she knew better than that. She was the one dangerous witness now. If he forced her out of here with him, she would not last long. Now she knew exactly where she stood. If only she knew the time! How long to nine o'clock and Dave calling for her? How long to the return of Chief Inspector Felse who had left, mysteriously, before noon? He would not leave his case unvetted overnight.

"You're coming," said Hugh very softly, "whether you choose to or not."

"How far?" said Dinah. "Where will you ditch me, Hugh? And how far do you think you'll get, afterwards? How's your passport, Hugh? Where will you get passage out? You don't know the professional routes, do you?"

"Dinah," he said, moving gently in upon the table that stood between me, "you used to love me—I know you loved me . . . "

"God!" she said, sick and furious with revulsion, "if you could only know how I despise you now! It isn't even the killing—it's the treachery—the *cowardice* . . . "

"Shut up!" he said in a muted scream that rasped his throat raw. "Shut up, or I'll kill you here and now . . ."

"Kill me, then! Fetch them in running! What will that do for you?"

He came on quietly, in cold control of himself again after that brief outburst. His thigh touched the rim of the table. Without taking his eyes from her or relaxing for an instant the steadiness of his aim at her body, he lowered his free hand, took the rim in his palm, and hoisted the table on one leg, wheeling it aside from between them. She moved promptly to circle with it as it swung, but he had manoeuvred her into a corner, and now she had nowhere to retreat from him.

She waited for him to move slowly round the rim towards her, and then suddenly she gripped the edge of the table with both hands and heaved it upright, aiming the coffee-pot at him. China and sugar and sandwiches went flying, the brass table-top struck him on the hip, but he stepped sharply back, hardly spattered, and the gun steadied again upon her. Hugh planted a foot deliberately in the wreckage and walked through it, crushing and breaking, his eyes never deflected from their aim.

"You're coming with me, Dinah, love, whether you want to or not. You're coming with me a little way . . ."

Her shoulders were flattened against the wall; she could not move any farther. His free hand came out, carefully, smoothly, and gripped her by the wrist.

The door opened, a small, prosaic, normal sound. Robert came quietly into the room and closed the door after him.

He looked as he always looked, pallid, colourless, calm, the very fibre of his clan, worn down to the essential substance but made to last for ever. He paused in the doorway to set his course, and after a moment of taking stock he began to move forward into the room. And everything went into slow motion and synchronised with his advancing steps.

Hugh dropped Dinah as if she counted for nothing; perhaps now she did. She squared her shoulders against the wall, and watched, helpless to do more. Everything had been taken out of her hands. Even the gun ignored her now, its minute, steely eye trained upon Robert.

But she was not quite forgotten, after all. Suddenly Hugh had remembered her mettle and taken her back into account. She saw that he was moving gradually aside, the gun never wavering, to work himself into a position where he could cover both of them, and no one could get behind him. Dinah moved, too, abruptly aware of the possibilities, stooping in one flashing movement to scoop up a knife from the wreckage of the table, and slide along the wall. But she had moved too late; she could not get out of his vision again, and he knew too much to shift his aim even for an instant, but still he was aware of what she did.

"Drop it, Dinah! On the tray, where I can hear!"

She could not risk the shot that would not even be fired at her. The knife tinkled back harmlessly among the fragments of china.

"Robert," said Hugh, softly and earnestly, "it isn't much I'm asking you for, this time. Not even to lie. Only a head start, that's all, just time to get away. Nothing new has happened—there needn't be any alarm. Just give me tonight, that's all I want. Just tonight—and your silence . . ."

Robert had halted, only a few steps into the room, when Hugh moved to put a wall at his back. Slowly he turned to face him directly again.

"Robert, I'm not asking you to do it for me. But won't you, for Mother's sake . . . ?"

It had been his trump card for years, but this time it fluttered ineffectively to the ground, and Robert's first advancing step trod it underfoot. The pale, calm face did not change at all.

"It won't work any more, Hugh. She's safe enough from you now. She's dead."

He halted for a moment, and looked at Dinah, and the fixed lines of his long, tired features softened briefly.

"Go home, Dinah. Just walk out now and take the car, and go. Leave me with him. He won't try to stop you." Hugh didn't move, didn't make a sound; for suddenly the only weapon he had was the tiny, deadly weapon in his hand, and for all its deadliness, suddenly it was not enough. It seemed to Dinah that she could indeed have walked straight out at the door then, between the two brothers, and got into the Mini and driven away. But she didn't move, either.

"Go, please, Dinah," said Robert gently. "I tried to tell you yesterday that you shouldn't so much as come near us, let alone ever think of tying yourself to one of us for life."

Hugh drew a long, careful breath. "I don't believe you. You're lying to me. She isn't dead, you're only trying to kid me into giving up . . ."

"She's dead, Hugh. Five or six minutes ago. I came down to telephone Braby. And I heard the table go over. Don't bet on her any more, Hugh. She's dead—it's finished."

He was walking forward slowly, measured step by step, and his eyes were fixed on Hugh's face with an unwavering purpose that matched the fixity of the gun's one minute black eye. And as he came he talked, quietly, coherently, without passion.

"Bad enough that I covered up one murder for

you, and kept you fed and indulged with money ever since, so that you'd never feel the need to kill again. Bad enough that I've acted as your grave-digger and watchman and nurse all this time, and caused another death, all to keep her from ever knowing what you and he between you have done to her name and her life—the only two people she ever cared about in the world. That's enough. It's all over now," said Robert clearly, "I can call things by their proper names now. You're a murderer and I'm an accessory. And we're both bastards. And she's dead! *Thank God!*"

Only a few feet separated them now, and still Hugh had not moved. Robert held out his hand with authority for the gun.

"Give that thing to me!"

"Keep off!" said Hugh loudly and violently. "Keep off and let me by, or I'll fire. I'm clearing out!"

"No, Hugh, you're not going anywhere. It's finished."

Dinah was distantly aware of a loud knocking that seemed to be within her head, for no one else heard it. Then she knew it for the knocker on the front door. The night nurse arriving? The police returning? Dave coming to fetch her home?

"Keep off, I warn you, or I'll kill you!"

And Robert smiled at him and came on, his hand extended. Dinah understood, a fraction of a second too late, that Robert had his own inviolable reason for moving in like this on an armed and desperate man, a proffered target closing and closing to pointblank range. All he wanted, at least in that moment, was to be dead and done with it, all that long purgatory of horror and disgust. Out in the hall there were men entering, the front door stood open; they would have seen this one subdued light, and it was here they were coming. But Robert did not want them to arrive in time.

Dinah saw the slight convulsion pass through Hugh's forearm and hand. She shrieked: "Hugh— *no!*" And perhaps it was her scream that diverted his attention at the very instant of firing, or perhaps in this face-to-face confrontation his hand shook in superstitious dread, and some last instinct in him tried subconsciously to turn the shot aside, for after all, this was his brother. The report of the shot closed with the echo of Dinah's scream, and Robert's tall body jerked a little backwards, folded slowly at the knees, and collapsed in an angular heap. And suddenly the room was full of men, Chief Inspector Felse and Sergeant Moon and half a dozen others, and Dave hard on their heels.

George Felse said afterwards that there was one moment when he gave Dinah Cressett up for dead, because she launched herself like fury straight between the police and the gun, which had still five serviceable rounds of .25 ACP ammunition in its eight-round magazine, as they afterwards confirmed. Dinah was not thinking of herself or of the police, or of the nearness or remoteness of her own death, but only intent on reaching Robert's body and feeling for the pulse and the heartbeat that were still alive in him.

But the moment passed without another tragedy; for Hugh, seeing the hopelessness of resistance, did the only thing left for him to do, and turned his little plaything upon himself.

This time he felt no superstitious terror, and his hand did not tremble. This time he made no mistake.

CHAPTER 14

THEY RUSHED Robert to hospital at emergency speed, siren blaring, and Comerbourne's chief surgeon spent most of the night getting the bullet out of the wreckage of his left shoulder and putting the pieces back together, which was rather like assembling a jigsaw puzzle. For so small a calibre it had done a lot of damage; if he got off without a long stay in an orthopaedic ward later, he'd be lucky, but there was a good chance of an eighty per cent recovery eventually.

"Lucky for him," said George to Sergeant Moon later, "that his father only brought back a Walther 8 from North Africa with him, instead of one of those 9 millimetre Lugers or something even bigger. A lot of the ranking officers in the German army carried those little fellows as auxiliary arms in the last war. I wonder how many of them are still running round loose in this country?"

They had the report from ballistics by then, and knew that the bullet recovered from Thomas Claybourne's skull had been fired from this particular Walther 8, as had the companion bullet extracted from the cellar door. They had the coat, and the button from Dinah's cardigan; they had a firm identification of the body of Thomas Claybourne, and understandable motive, everything necessary to a clear, satisfactory case. Except someone to charge.

"Ah, and so much the better," said Sergeant Moon. "Saves the country's money, makes sure he never does it again, and obviates any resultant harm and distress to innocent parties, which couldn't do anybody any good, not even the great British public.''

"Innocent?'' murmured George. They were sitting side by side in a settle at the ''Duck'', in the quiet late morning hours when they had the place to themselves.

Diplomatically, Sergeant Moon did not answer. Mrs. Macsen-Martel was dead, the vicar himself was taking charge of her funeral arrangements, and the village had become a kind of closed shop, deceptively talkative except when strangers presumed to join in or even listen to the talk, when it was found to be designed only to avoid imparting information, to derail questions before they ever got asked, and to deploy a smoke-screen in which the more persistent could smother or withdraw.

"There isn't going to be any trial, only a statement closing the case,'' mused the sergeant, "and they won't get much out of that. So technically we can hardly plead that anything's *sub judice*—unless you're contemplating other charges?''

"And if they start pumping you like that in here tonight,'' George asked with interest, "what do you say?''

"We say we can't discuss it, it's *sub judice*,'' said the sergeant without hesitation. "By the time they realise those possible other charges aren't going to material-ise, they've lost interest anyhow, and gone off after some new horror. Five hundred miles away, let's hope!''

"All right, that's my answer, too. It's going to be days, in any case, before I can even question him. I'm certainly not going to rush the doctors on this one. And if he's going to be a hospital case for weeks, maybe months, afterwards, time is hardly of the essence.''

"And will you be needing a shorthand writer when you do see him, George?"

"Now you come to mention it, Jack, I don't believe I shall. A short written statement later, perhaps, just to round out my report."

"Ah, that's the spirit," said Sergeant Moon with a gratified sigh. "If you want any help with the editing, I'll be glad to come along and lend a hand."

The village knew, but the village, which knew so well how to disseminate information, knew also how to keep its own counsel. The reporters came with cameras, loitered, questioned, even extracted answers, which were only later seen to be either useless or mutually destructive. There was a large and impressive funeral, to which the whole valley came as a gesture of solidarity, not with the Macsen-Martel clan as such, but with its own people. Later, when the inquest was over and permission given, there would be another and quieter funeral, which those whose official duty it was would attend, and from which the rest would turn their eyes decently away, out of a discretion which nobody had to dictate. Even the inquest would not bring the newsmen very much joy, only the eyewitnesses' evidence and the bald fact of a verdict of suicide. And the case would be closed. No trial, no conviction; never, officially, a murderer.

"She was a game old girl," said Saul Trimble, when the regulars mustered in the bar of the "Duck" after the burial, still black-clad and sombre and exclusive, so like a private wake that all those who were not in the inner circle took one look within, and retired to the garden bar. "A game old girl, and never owed a penny."

The valley had a gift for epitaphs. But it was Sam Crouch who found the only possible one for Hugh, late in the evening when the clock was ticking its way round to closing-time.

"Ah, well, he was his father's son," said Sam, wagging his round, simple, good-natured head.

Eb Jennings swivelled a rapid glance from Sam to Ellie, who had just dropped a glass into the washing-up bowl with an almighty splash that swamped the floor behind the bar. "You can say *that* again!"

"Nice-looking, though, you got to admit," said Nobbie regretfully, mentally reviewing the revised list of interesting males. "Seems awful now, but you know, there were times when I rather fancied Hugh!"

There was, thought Ellie, industriously mopping up the spilled water, always a bright side to everything.

It was a week before Robert was allowed to fill in what gaps were left in the story. He had offered earlier, and his offer had been first vetoed by the doctors, and then courteously deprecated by the police, whose behaviour throughout had been so considerate as almost to offend against his standards. When George finally came to sit beside his bed in the private ward borrowed for the occasion, Robert was propped up on carefully stacked pillows, his left shoulder completely encased in plaster and bandages. He had lost weight he could not afford to lose, and his pallor was so fine-drawn as to make him practically translucent, but his eyes were peaceful and resigned.

"I'm only sorry," said George, "that I was rather later than I intended getting back that night. But I wasn't expecting anything to break, and if Miss Cressett hadn't dropped her bombshell, nothing would have."

Robert's face kept its guarded stillness at the mention of Dinah's name. "I don't know that I was too grateful to you, at first, for turning up at all,'' he said frankly.

"Never mind, you may have good reason to be grateful later,'' said George equably. "I knew by then it was your brother we wanted. He was a shade too clever about worming his way into the cellar, so I thought, well, all right, let him, let's see what happens. He dropped his bit of evidence against you in the only place he could get at easily, covering the action with his handkerchief. He couldn't know that we'd been sifting cleared soil back into that pit for more than an hour then, so if there was anything new to be found by going through that layer again, it was plain he must have put it there. If he could have dropped it into the heap of soil on the far side of the cellar, which hadn't been sieved, then he'd have had a better chance of getting away with it. Though even then probably thinner than he realised. He was just that little bit too anxious. Before I went north I told Brice to go carefully over the floor of the trench again. And when he confronted you with the pencil, and you owned it for yours at once—well, we knew then who was our man. I'm afraid that piece of cold-blooded treachery hit you harder than anything.''

Robert's fastidious face had tightened into extreme pain even at the recollection, he flinched at every accusatory word levelled against Hugh, but he did not protest.

"So I came back prepared to stick my neck out and charge him, and worry afterwards about all the supporting details. But Miss Cressett beat us to it. And now suppose you tell your side of the story.''

It was what Robert had been bracing himself to do for days. "Shouldn't there be someone to record what I say?''

"No, there should not. I haven't cautioned you, and at present there's no question of doing anything of the kind. Just talk, if you feel like talking. Tonight you don't need a solicitor."

And Robert talked.

"It was five years ago, a day early in March, I think, when this man Claybourne came to the Abbey asking for me. He knew about the family my father had left from the obituary, I suppose. My mother happened to be away for a week-end, which was luck, because it didn't happen very often. The man had taken a bus straight from the station at Comerbourne, and got off at the end of our lane, so hardly anyone can even have seen him. He had his luggage with him, and he had a copy of his mother's wedding group and certificate, his birth certificate, everything he needed to prove his legitimacy. What he wanted was money. He wasn't an offensive type, really, rather anxious and harassed, he didn't want me to think of his demands as blackmail, and he didn't want to press his claims to the issue, all he was after was as much cash as possible. The last thing he wanted was anything to do with law or the police. I got the impression that he was in a hurry to get away somewhere for reasons of his own.

"But there wasn't any money to give him. My father's—*our* father's—debts weren't yet cleared, and there was never much cash to spare. I couldn't see anything for it but to go with him to our solicitor and tell the whole story, and get his advice about how to arrange things as justly as possible, and with the least shock to my mother. *He* wanted money and no fuss, *I* wanted my mother's peace of mind let alone. I thought maybe we could find some way of raising a loan, since that was what he preferred, too.

"Only in the middle of all this, Hugh came home."

He paused to moisten his lips. In a sense this was the most terrible moment of all, for if Hugh had not come in at that point there need never have been any crime, or any long and hideous purgatory after it.

"I had to let him into it, too, he wanted to know who this person was. And he was furious. He wouldn't hear of paying, wouldn't let the solicitor into it or promise to keep the police out, to him it was plain blackmail. And yet he saw the proofs, just as I did, and he knew they must be genuine. After all, what was surprising in it, except the fact that he found it necessary to marry her? We'd known many other cases, only different in that one particular. But that was the one that mattered. Maybe we hadn't got much left to boast about, or to spend, but what there was Hugh was going to keep, and his name was his and was going to stay his.

"Claybourne was frightened. He couldn't afford delay or inquiry, he was desperately anxious to placate us, he swore he hadn't told a soul where he was coming, he hadn't any intention of ever asserting his right to the name, and nothing could ever possibly leak out, because no one else knew. All he wanted was money. And Hugh laughed with relief—genuine relief, you understand—and said that made everything simple. He went off into the old library—we were standing in the hall—as though he'd thought of something helpful. But what he came back with was the gun.

"You've seen it. You know all about that. My father brought it home after the war, and he and Hugh used to practise at a target with it sometimes. Hugh was quite good. I haven't good enough vision, and anyhow, I wasn't interested. Even then I was slow to realise what was happening, or I might have prevented it. Claybourne was quicker. He simply took one look, and cast round for somewhere to run to. Hugh was coming down the stairs, between him and the door. He did what I suppose one would

naturally do, ran towards that big window at the back
of the hall, that looks as if it ought to have a door in it.
But it hasn't, when you get close you see how the
ground slopes away outside. He looked round for
some way of escape, and saw the light falling through
the high window in the cellar, just at the foot of the
stairs. You know it. It looks as if there must be a way
out there.''

"But there isn't any way out. Yes, I know.''

"And even the cellar door was locked—not that it
would have made any difference, he couldn't get
away. I blame myself," he said, "for being so slow to
believe in what I was seeing. But when you've lived
all your life with someone—one of your family—and
always thought of him as a normal human being . . .
By the time I realised this was in earnest, Hugh was
past me, I ran after him, but he was half way down
the cellar steps, and all that happened when I caught
hold of his arm was that the gun went off and the shot
went wide—into the door. And Hugh turned round
and hit me in the face. I was off-balance, and I went
down sprawling on the stairs. And Hugh walked on
down, not even hurrying, and fired again at close
range. In the head. Just like throwing a dart in a pub
match.

"When I got there, the man was dead. Stone dead.
Nobody was ever going to bring him back again. And
Hugh was saying, what the hell are you fussing about,
it's *all right*, nobody knows he ever came here, there's
nothing to worry about, everything's fine. Everything's fine. And Hugh was always her favourite son.
And anyhow, it was done. How do you make
amends?

"So I buried him. Him and all his belongings, all
but the documents he'd brought with him, his wallet
—all those things Hugh took and burned. My mother
never knew anything. Never! Thank God!

"And I've been in hell ever since."

It was a simple statement, made in the interests of accuracy, not at all a complaint, much less an appeal for sympathy.

"Not Hugh, of course. He got a bit restive about being in the same house, afterwards, so he shrugged the whole thing off and went somewhere else, got himself a home and a job, even fell a little in love, I think—as much as he could with anyone but himself. As far as I know he was quite happy. Maybe there was just something vital left out of him. He even levered money out of me from time to time, in return for his discretion and good behaviour. I thought if I kept him content, nothing else might happen, never again. But of course it did. I thought maybe it was only a monstrous aberration, something he'd never really registered properly, and he'd grow out of it . . . " Robert's long, sensitive lips curled in the most rueful of smiles. He heaved a long sigh, and was silent for a moment.

"She was not a lovable person, my mother," he said at length, choosing his words with scrupulous care, "and I wasn't very attached to her, any more than she was to me. But I respected and admired her. She had standards I shared. And she loved Hugh. And she didn't deserve *that*! What else could I have done?"

He needed no answer from George, and George offered none. And in a moment Robert resumed strongly:

"I'd tried at first to get the bullet out, but it was impossible without doing much more damage, so I left it alone and just plugged the hole and varnished over it. But you wouldn't credit how visible that spot still was to me. It seemed to get more obvious every time I looked at it, and I looked often. Touching it up only seemed to make it show up worse. I thought of a knocker, as one way of hiding it for good. I had to hunt round for some months before I found one from much the same period, at an antique shop in Brighton. My mother never went into the cellar, or I should have had to tell her some story to account for it, and that would have been awkward, because later I had to concoct another story to cover a much wider field, and I doubt if I should have had the luck to make all the details fit. But she didn't go, and she didn't see it, and there wasn't any problem, not then.

"Only the time came when we simply couldn't carry the burden of the house any longer. We had to get a grant, or something of the kind, and these negotiations with the National Trust began, and then I saw that the door would have to go. I never could get the flags back properly, it would have given everything away. We were going to be dealing with meticulous experts, and if they had a fine original door there, then it would have to be put into as near perfect order as possible. I was afraid they might want to relay the flags. So all I could think of was to make up that tale about the south porch of the church, and if there wasn't much evidence for it, there wasn't any to disprove it. When it came to the point, my mother wasn't any problem. I had only to tell her that my father had once told me the story as a family tradition— the sort of thing he laughed about, but might occasionally trot out to amuse the children—and she accepted it as gospel, as she always did everything that came from him, however false. I said we'd happened on the knocker once among a lot of junk in what used to be the tack-room in the stable block, and he'd told me it belonged to this door, and said in his casual way that it—door, knocker and all—ought to be in the church porch if everybody had his rights, and some day he'd put it back there. That was enough for her. Whatever *he* had suggested, however frivolously, was sacred law to her.''

"And the other story," said George, "the one about the monk found dead, burned by the sanctuary knocker—you made that up, too, didn't you? Hoping Miss Cressett would pass it on, as she did.''

"I had to. I knew someone else was going to be found dead there very soon. Hugh had just told me. He had a car to deliver that evening, and when he doubled back on foot through the churchyard he found this photographer . . . Hugh was always quick to grasp the immediate implications . . . and crazily quick to act. He never looked beyond.''

"And you, as usual, were supposed to provide cover for him,'' George said. 'And for your mother's sake you tried.''

The pale lips tightened painfully. Robert was averse to any appearance of making excuses. "I'm sorry I put it like that. What I've done I've done, and I prefer to pay. It makes me even more ashamed that I made use of Dinah. I told you, I blame myself, no one else. But I was at the end of my tether then, to think it was all repeating itself, and all my fault.''

"All, Robert?''

"I was responsible—I mean a responsible person. He was not.''

It seemed as good a division of humanity into two significant halves as any other, George thought, but it was hard on those who located themselves in the half that carries the burdens. He looked down soberly at the pale, drained face on the pillow, and totted up in his own mind the number of charges he could bring, if he so chose, against this responsible person who would never deny one count out of all the possible counts with which society could accuse him. Concealing a death, accessory after the fact of murder, harbouring—why go on? There was a scapegoat handy who could save society a good deal of money and scandal, and Robert a prolonged refinement of suffering. Hugh had killed, let Hugh bury the dead, too, Hugh who had never lifted anyone else's load in his life. It might count almost as virtue to him if after death he was made to bear Robert's share of this as well as his own.

"You'll want an official statement from me," said Robert, "about all this. I'll make it whenever you think fit."

George thought fit that some judicious editing should be done on the story before it took any official form, but he did not say so. There is such a thing as a justice which dispenses with law—when it has the rare chance that hurts nobody and benefits many. In any case, Robert was going to spend weeks, probably months, under orthopaedic treatment.

"I shall need only a short statement to include in my report. I'll prepare a text and read it to you—in a few days, there's no hurry now. Obviously there isn't going to be any trial, you see. You needn't worry about anything. I hope I haven't tired you out too much— "

"Not at all, Chief Inspector," said the incorrigibly polite, dutiful, obstinate lips, pale with strain.

"Good, then I think as Sister hasn't been after my blood so far, I might venture to send her in for a few minutes. You've got another visitor waiting."

Dinah came to the bedside quietly and gravely, and sat down with a composure which was not maintained without effort and anxiety. She saw, but did not choose to see, the flickering succession of emotions that passed over Robert's face, astonishment, alarm, dismay, despair, longing, hope, the resolute and heroic rejection of hope. Even when the face closed up on her and sealed itself like a sealed door, she declined to remember anything except the brief glimpse of longing, and the even briefer coruscation of hope, quenched implacably as soon as it was born.

"Hullo!" she said. "They told me I could have just ten minutes. I had to see for myself that you really were going to be all right." She had insisted on travelling with him in the ambulance that night, though herself, so they told her afterwards, in a mild state of shock, quiet, practical, determined and in nobody's way, Dinah suddenly grown up in an hour. An experience like that is going to leave its mark; it had left Dinah extended, enlightened, a person completed, mature enough to know all too well that her losses had not been great, and to turn a shrewd, honest, even predatory eye upon her gains. How curious! She had never once hunted Hugh, never for a moment been jealous of him!

"I'm quite all right," said Robert in a tightly controlled voice, "thank you. It was very kind of you to come."

He had recovered a little colour from somewhere, his thin face was suffused, even his spiky hair, dry as quills, had acquired a kind of vivacity in her presence, insisted on bristling in an awkward, almost a boyish manner.

"Dave drove me into town," she said, "they're waiting for me in the car park." She had to keep talking, or something would break. "They'll only let in one person at a time to see you. Dave plans on marrying his Alix next Spring. I thought you might like to know that some good came out of all this. In other circumstances he'd never have met her."

She was busy unwrapping the small parcel she had brought with her, and his eyes, for all their unhappiness, could not help following the movements of her fingers.

"I brought you this—look! I wanted to find

something permanent for you, not just flowers. Did I guess right?'' She had gone to a lot of trouble to find what she wanted, not even knowing what it would be until she found it, but knowing it with certainty when she did find it. Hospital toys should be special, intensely personal to both the giver and the receiver, and if possible inexhaustible. She had not even realised until now why she was so set on finding the right gift for him, never having considered gifts as a paradoxical mark of proprietorship.

She set the little painted box on the edge of his bed, and lifted the lid, and the minute powdered musician at the minute spinet within began to make jerky little movements to the tinkling strains of an early Mozart minuet, the notes sweet and fine-drawn as spun sugar. It would have gone on playing for three of their ten minutes, but he was too weak to endure it for so long. He quivered feebly in his plaster, and turned his head away. He was not, in his own view, the kind of person she should be approaching, with her clarity and youth and candour. The darkness in his own memory, the bitterness in his own experience, stood like a vast wall between them.

''You shouldn't have come,'' he said.

''Don't you like it?'' she asked disingenuously. The musical-box continued to spin sparkling strands of sugar. ''It isn't a new one, it's early nineteenth-century. Don't you think they did this sort of thing better then?''

He reached a hand out blindly, found the little box and closed the lid upon it, cutting off the end of the minuet. But he did it with a wild tenderness that was very revealing. ''You know it's lovely . . . you know I . . . '' He waited fully twenty seconds, motionless and rigid with effort, to regain control of his voice; she recognised that relentless patience in him.

''Dinah, you mustn't come here again. You

shouldn't have come now. Much better for you not to know me, I've done you enough harm—I and my family. You must realise that I'm a criminal. There are very serious counts against me, it's inevitable that I shall be charged . . .''

She said not a word about the doubts she held on that score. All she said was: ''I don't mind that. It makes no difference to me.''

''But it does to me. I tried to tell you, that day . . . I couldn't let you go ahead and link your life . . . I know I gave you a false impression, I was very clumsy. I wanted to warn you not to waste your youth and warmth and goodness on a Macsen-Martel— to steer clear of us as you would of the plague . . . ''

''But you're *not* a Macsen-Martel,'' said Dinah bluntly.

He was shaken out of his resolute despair as rudely as out of his feudal dream of responsibility. It was salutary. He lay in astonished silence and passivity for a long moment, and then he began to laugh. Rather precariously, because his physical state was still very low, but so gently that she felt no need to hush and soothe him out of it. It ran through him like a life-giving pulse.

''Oh, Dinah, I'd forgotten,'' he said, quaking with the first pure mirth of years, ''I'd quite forgotten I'm a bastard. It's true, my mother's maiden name came straight out of the commercial midlands—grand-mother was the Martel who married money. Do you know what that makes me now? Plain Robert Smith!''

He laughed himself, predictably, into tears of weakness. She wanted to touch him, to reassure him, to involve him once for all and drive him farther along the road on which she had already started him; she wanted to open the lid of the musical-box again and set her seal on him as shamelessly as if she had put a

ring on his finger, or in his nose. But she did none of
these things. The ten minutes were up, and he'd had
enough for one day. And she knew how to be patient,
too.

"And what's the matter with Smith for a name?"
said Dinah mildly. And she patted his nearer hand—
it was clasped very firmly over her gift—and walked
confidently out of the ward.